The group captain looked long and hard at Yeoman, and was inwardly pleased by the enthusiasm which the pilot made no attempt to hide.

'It will be dangerous and exacting work,' he continued, 'and now perhaps you have an inkling of why you were chosen for this job. We needed someone with a thorough knowledge of German fighter procedures and tactics; someone who has fought the enemy in every theatre. That someone was you. For the time being, you will be in overall command of the Wing.'

'I may as well tell you that a new Group is soon to be formed for the specific task of bomber support; that is to say intruder and countermeasures work against the enemy air defences. The Burningham Wing will pioneer the techniques which, we hope, will form the basis of a highly efficient and elite force—a force whose aim will be to confound and destroy.

'Well, that's about it. Do you have any questions?'

Yeoman stood up, picking up his cap from the chair arm.

'Just one, sir,' he said. 'When do we start?'

Also by Robert Jackson

FIGHTER ACES OF WORLD WAR II
HURRICANE SQUADRON
SQUADRON SCRAMBLE
TARGET TOBRUK
MALTA VICTORY

and published by Corgi Books

Mosquito Squadron
Yeoman in the battle over Germany

Robert Jackson

CORGI BOOKS

A DIVISION OF TRANSWORLD PUBLISHERS LTD

MOSQUITO SQUADRON

A CORGI BOOK 0 552 11987 3

Originally published in Great Britain by Arthur Barker Ltd.

PRINTING HISTORY
Arthur Barker edition published 1981
Corgi edition published 1982

This book is set in Times Roman 10 on 11 pt.

Corgi Books are published by Transworld Publishers Ltd., Century House, 61–63 Uxbridge Road, Ealing, London, W5 5SA

Printed in Great Britain by
Hunt Barnard Printing Ltd., Aylesbury, Bucks.

Chapter One

IT HAD BEEN A LONG, HOT DAY, AND THE OLD MAN WAS VERY tired. Every jolt of the cart sent new aches through his bones, and although the sun had now set and the air was cooler, clouds of midges continued to plague him.

He stared moodily at the backside of his patient, plodding old mare. Her patchy coat was grimed with coal dust, as was the old man himself. The sway of her body between the cart shafts registered protest and he gave her an affectionate flick with his long stick, dislodging a cluster of flies which seemed intent on bedding down for the night.

'Not long now, old girl,' he muttered encouragingly. 'Soon be home now.'

It wasn't fair, he complained inwardly, to make them work until such an hour. Why, it was only a matter of months ago that Schneider, the coal merchant for whom they worked (the old man always considered himself and his mare as partners) had put the pair of them out to grass. No longer of any use in a mechanized age: that was the expression the pompous ass had used. Well, here they were, back in harness again, because Schneider had come begging with cap in hand after the authorities had requisitioned his fine new-fangled trucks to move supplies destined for the troops on the Russian front up to the docks in Hamburg.

The old man glanced over to his right, across the miles

of flat, low-lying ground and the great expanse of the Elbe estuary towards the old Hanseatic seaport—the second largest in the world, or so they said. Dieter had told him about that. He smiled with inward pride as he thought of his only son; Dieter knew all about such things, for he was a clever lad who had been top of his class in college. The old man wished that he had had the benefit of such an education, for he wouldn't now be staring at the coal-streaked posterior of a horse. At least that was one good thing Hitler had achieved; he had given the youth of Germany the chance to be educated, no matter what background they came from.

Educated, he thought with sudden bitterness, to be pitch-forked into this crazy war. He had fought in the previous one, and he knew that the real losers were the poor bastards who had to do the fighting, no matter what side they were on. Like the twin sons of his neighbour, Widow Mengel, swallowed up with the Sixth Army at Stalingrad along with ninety thousand others. Hardly a family in Germany had been untouched by that catastrophe, and it had been quickly followed by another: the collapse of the Axis armies in North Africa. Then, only a few days ago, had come the news that the British and Americans had landed in Sicily. The newspapers said that the Allies were being pushed back into the sea, but the old man didn't believe them, although he never said as much to anyone, not even to the few close friends with whom he smoked a pipe twice a week in the Red Hen just down the road from his little house on the outskirts of Stade. Talking too much could be dangerous, and the old man wanted to go on smoking his pipe and drinking a few steins in the Red Hen for a few more years to come.

His thoughts turned to Dieter once again. At least the boy was safe enough, commanding a flak battery on the outskirts of Paris and having a pretty good time there, by all accounts. One of the old man's greatest regrets was that the German Army had never got as far as Paris in the last war; but the next generation had got there all right, and the cognac Dieter brought home during his leaves was more than welcome as a change from the Red Hen's beer.

In fact, reflected the old man, Dieter was probably safer

than most of the folks at home. The air raids were getting worse. The Tommies, who came at night, had been bad enough, but now the Amis were coming over in daylight, and the Luftwaffe didn't seem able to stop them. What was it fatty Goering had said, back in '39, in one of his radio broadcasts? 'If an enemy plane ever flies over the territory of the Reich, you can call me Meyer.' Yes, that was it, or something like it. Well, thought the old man, I'll bet those poor devils in Essen and the other Ruhr towns are calling him Meyer now, and a few other names besides.

The old man let the mare have her head while he fished out a battered pipe and tamped some tobacco into it. Searching his pockets, he found a box of matches, struck one and touched it to the bowl, carefully shielding the flame in his cupped hands. These days, one could be locked up for showing any kind of light after sunset.

Puffing contentedly, he tapped the weary mare with his stick, urging her to move faster. There was still a good deal of daylight left, and with luck they would be home before dark. He didn't like to arrive back after nightfall, because his wife worried about him and her heart was by no means strong; there was no sense in causing her unnecessary anxiety.

In any case, he didn't like to linger on this stretch of the road. He preferred to look straight ahead and pass along it as quickly as possible, past the tall fence with its concrete posts and barbed wire, the long, low mound beyond it, the gate and the armed sentries. He did not know what went on in there, nor did he want to; in fact, he could not even hazard a guess. There were a lot of aerials around the bunker, sticking up like skeletal fingers, but what purpose they served he had no means of knowing.

The guards were there as usual. He knew most of them by sight, and somehow they had found out his name. One of them called out to him as he drew abreast.

'Why, it's old Kurt, the coalman. Long past your bedtime, old codger. Hurry along home, now. The Tommies might be over tonight.'

The old man spat into the road. 'Then you'd better keep that thick skull of yours under cover, hadn't you?' he grunted.

7

The sentry laughed and watched as the old man trundled on his way, leaving an acrid smell of sweat and pungent tobacco behind him. Overhead, the stars were beginning to come out, showing briefly through rifts in the cloud that was drifting slowly in from the sea across Lower Saxony.

Beneath the long mound, protected by fifty feet of earth and reinforced concrete, lay the great underground operations room of the Luftwaffe's 2nd Air Division. The room was bisected by a huge sheet of frosted glass; on it, overlaid with a grid, was an outline map of Germany, the Low Countries and part of the North Sea. On the other side of the screen, behind small individual desks, sat twenty or so Luftwaffe women auxiliaries; each girl wore a headset and was in direct contact with one of the big 'Freya' warning radar stations that stretched in a great arc along the north-west coast of Germany, down through Holland and into Belgium.

In front of each girl, meticulously checked and rechecked to ensure that it was in full working order, was a small projector. As soon as a report of an incoming raid was received from one of the coastal radar units, she would project a spot of light on to the appropriate square of the grid. The spot could be varied in size to indicate the strength of the attackers to the fighter controllers across the room.

The latter sat in two long rows directly in front of the screen. Behind them, on a raised dais, was the position reserved for the Divisional Commander or his deputy. On this occasion the big chief, Lieutenant-General Schwabedissen, was present in person, flanked by liaison officers from the various fighter units under his command. There was another identical operations room in Germany, at Döberitz near Berlin, a third at Metz, in France, and a fourth at Deelen near Arnhem, in Holland, all in constant touch with one another. Between them, they were responsible for the air defence of the Third Reich by day and night.

Seated third from the left at the end of one of the rows of liaison officers, Major Joachim Richter sighed deeply and felt a craving for one of the long cigars he had taken to smoking recently, but smoking in the operations room was strictly forbidden. It was a pity, for a smoke might have relaxed some of the tension; the air was electric with it. Apart from the whirring of electric fans and an occasional nervous cough, there was almost complete silence. It was always like this when a raid was known to be building up; already, radar stations on the Belgian coast had detected what appeared to be large formations of bombers assembling over East Anglia, but they had not yet set course and so far there was no indication of which route they would take, or what their target would be. All the fighter controllers could do now was wait, together with the night fighter crews who were at readiness throughout Germany and Occupied Europe.

It was over five months now since Richter's unit, Jagdgeschwader (Fighter Wing) 66 had been pulled out of Sicily, from where it had taken part in the great air battles over Malta, and brought back to Germany to take part in the defence of the Reich. Richter's mind went back to the summer of 1942 and to a conversation with an old friend, a Stuka dive-bomber pilot named Conrad Seliger, soon after JG 66's arrival at Catania. Things had seemed rosy enough then, with Rommel's Afrika Korps heading flat out for Cairo and an invasion of Malta on the cards, but a few short months had been enough to shatter all Axis hopes of a victory in the Mediterranean. Malta had never been invaded, and her warships and bombers had continued to strangle Rommel's supply lines until, after a wild chase all the way back across the Western Desert, the Afrika Korps had been crushed to extinction between the nutcrackers of the British and American armies in Tunisia. Now, using Malta and the newly-captured Tunisian bases as a springboard, the Allies had gone ashore in Sicily, and Richter had seen enough official reports on the situation to know that there was almost no hope of holding them there. The only logical thing to do, he thought, was to abandon the island and adopt a strong defensive posture in Italy, where the mountainous terrain did not favour the attacking forces.

But that was someone else's problem. It was here, over Germany, that the Luftwaffe's greatest battles would be fought, and Richter yearned to be in the thick of them. Fighter

Wing 66, after a short rest and re-equipment with new Messerschmitt 109Gs—'Iron Gustavs', as the pilots nicknamed them—had been in action almost continuously since its homecoming, operating out of Zwischenahn, and already some of the pilots had scored notable victories against the American B-17 Flying Fortresses attacking Wilhelmshaven and other north German ports.

Richter, however, had seen no combat since the days in Sicily. Instead, he had received immediate promotion to Major and had been temporarily withdrawn from operations; this subterranean vault had been his home for four months now.

Normally, Richter was assigned to the day shift, and despite his frustration at not being allowed into action he was forced to admit that the job had its compensations, foremost among which was the little nurse in Stade. Three times a week she finished work at six-thirty, just in time to get back to her apartment and have a meal ready for when he came off duty. She had been making determined attempts to have him move in with her, but so far he had resisted successfully. Both of them were having a pretty good time, but he had no intention of being trapped. There were still a lot of wild oats to be sown.

Richter was glad he was not a family man, like his friend Captain Wolfgang Lutz. Lutz's wife was expecting a child at any moment, and so Richter had agreed to take the captain's place on the night shift so that the man could be free to pace up and down the corridors of the maternity hospital in Hamburg. Richter smiled to himself, visualizing Lutz's bald head glistening with the anxiety of impending fatherhood, and resolved not to put himself in that sort of situation for a long time to come.

Richter glanced at the illuminated wall clock. The hands showed 2245, and beneath them the date glowed boldly in the dimly-lit room: 24 July 1943. Perhaps, thought Richter, the Tommies won't be over tonight, and realized at once that he was deluding himself. The weather forecast was good, with a moon and partial cloud cover up to 22,000 feet all the way across the North Sea. They would be on their way, all right. It was too much to hope that the radar reports of bomb-

10

ers assembling over the east coast of England were incorrect.

A few minutes later, the first spot of light appeared on one of the squares on the left-hand edge of the map. More appeared as the minutes went by and further radar reports came in, until the whole bore a striking similarity to a stream of glowing ants, crawling steadily eastwards. Two light spots, of lower intensity than the rest, were some distance ahead; Richter knew that these would be the pathfinders, their bomb-bays full of incendiaries and target markers.

The operations room now hummed with activity, as the women auxiliaries translated the constant stream of radar information into dancing slivers of light on the big map. Telephone bells shrilled and the room was filled with a confused babel of voices as the controllers and their liaison officers issued instructions to the waiting night fighters, anti-aircraft concentrations and civil defence organizations throughout 2nd Air Division's sector. Richter drummed his fingertips absent-mindedly on his desk top, eyeing the crawling stream of incoming bombers and wondering which direction it would ultimately take. His task was to liaise with the night fighter units in the Bremen area; these were to be held in reserve for the time being, until the ultimate direction of the enemy bomber stream was ascertained.

Already, some night fighters were on station off the north German coast, circling out over the sea beyond the Frisian Islands. The night fighters were mostly twin-engined Messerschmitt 110s; each one assigned to an individual zone, the zones overlapping to form a long chain extending from the Baltic to Belgium. The fighters were controlled by 'Wurzburg' tracking radars, which took over from the 'Freya' early warning chain as the bombers approached German territory and fed information on courses, heights and speeds to the fighter controllers. The latter would bring the night fighters into contact with the bomber stream, and after that it was up to the radar operators in the Messerschmitts to locate individual bombers with their 'Lichtenstein' airborne interception radars and steer their pilots to within firing range.

Each one of the overlapping fighter sectors had a code-name—Hamster, Butterfly, Herring, Polar Bear, Jaguar, Tiger and so on. Together, they were the front line of a deep air defence system of fighters, searchlights and anti-aircraft guns, devised and put into operation more than two years earlier by General Josef Kammhumber, the Luftwaffe's night fighter commander. The fighter zones, each with a radius of about fifty miles, were code-named 'Sky Bed' collectively and they had worked well enough in 1941, when the RAF's night bombers were attacking in small numbers. But in the middle of 1943, with the bombers coming over in their hundreds, it was a different story.

Richter looked at the wall clock again. It was ten minutes after midnight, and over his headset he could hear the controllers steering the outer screen of fighters towards their first contacts.

'Tiger, Tiger, couriers in sector Dora-Bertholdt, course zero-eight-zero, height Anton two-nine...couriers in Dora-Dora, zero-eight-five, Anton two-two...' And so it went on as the minutes ticked by, in jargon meaningless to all but trained ears, as the Messerschmitts climbed through the darkness, carrying two young men barely out of school in each of their cockpits, to a deadly rendezvous high over the North Sea with the Lancasters and Halifaxes of the RAF, each carrying seven young men barely out of school.

At twenty minutes past midnight, with the first contacts now expected at any moment, the head of the crawling stream of luminous ants on the big screen was precisely at position 54 degrees 10 minutes north, 07 degrees 30 minutes east, or twenty miles west of Heligoland. Richter listened intently, waiting for the first *'Pauke, pauke'*—the 'Tally Ho!' of the German night fighters—that would herald the first kills of the night. His practised eye took in the spattering of smaller dots on the screen, each one representing a friendly fighter; it looked as though the ones from Sector Jaguar would be the first to intercept.

Eighteen thousand feet over the German Bight, crouched over the cathode ray tube of his Lichtenstein AI set, Warrant Officer Hans Dorfmann of No. 2 Night Fighter Wing was elatedly chasing the biggest, fattest contact he had ever made in his eighteen months as a radar observer. Slowly and very precisely, striving to keep the excitement out of his voice, he steered his pilot, Lieutenant Stechel, towards it.

'Four kilometres . . . course zero-one-zero . . . zero-one-five now . . . hold her on zero-one-five . . . ease her up two hundred metres . . .'

This was beautiful. He was bringing Stechel right up under the bomber's tail. In the front cockpit, the pilot was already searching the sky ahead, his fingers curled around the triggers that would release a lethal stream of cannon shells and machine-gun bullets from the Messerschmitt 110's nose armament into the wings and fuselage of their target.

Seconds later, Dorfmann's curse burst over the intercom, his voice high-pitched with frustration.

'Damn it, my set has packed in! Lost contact!'

In front of his eyes, the hitherto clear image on his screen had suddenly dissolved into a spider's web of confused, shimmering lines, totally incomprehensible.

Stechel, too, felt a deep surge of disappointment. 'Try and get it working,' he ordered the observer. 'I'll carry out a visual search. The bastard can't be far away.'

Dorfmann juggled with the controls of his radar, but it was hopeless. To judge from the crazy echoes on his screen, it was as though the bomber they had been following had suddenly reproduced itself into dozens of aircraft, surging this way and that across the sky.

In the operations room at Stade, frantic messages were received one after the other from the 'Wurzburg' ground control radars and from the fighters they had been directing. Everywhere it was the same story: the radar echoes had crumbled into shifting, meaningless bands of light on every screen in and above northern Germany.

Joachim Richter leaned back in his seat, staring at the big glass screen on which the orderly, moving spots of light had now come to a standstill.

'I don't believe it,' he muttered. 'I just don't bloody well believe it.'

Yet it was true. Somehow, incredibly, the enemy had succeeded in blinding the radar eyes of the German air defences—eyes without which the night fighters could not be directed to their targets and the flak batteries could not lay their guns accurately. There was no means, now, of telling which way the bomber stream was heading, until it actually crossed the coast and its progress was reported by observers on the ground.

High over the German Bight, Lieutenant Stechel brought his Messerschmitt 110 round in a wide circle above the clouds. He knew that he must be right in the middle of the bomber stream, but despite the moonlight he could see no other aircraft.

Suddenly, he stood the fighter on its wingtip, pulling it round in a steep turn and bringing a startled exclamation from Dorfmann, still fiddling with his set behind him.

'Sorry about that,' Stechel gasped, levelling the wings. 'Look outside. What do you make of that?'

At first, Dorfmann thought that the 110 was flying through a snowstorm. The aircraft was surrounded by a blizzard of strange particles, glittering in the moonlight. One of them whirled close past the cockpit canopy and it looked, in the fraction of a second before it was lost to sight, like a long strip of metallic toilet paper.

The observer opened his mouth to speak, and in that instant Stechel slammed open the throttles, pulling the Messerschmitt into a steep climb. Ahead and above, his keen eyes had picked out a shadow, fleeting across the stars.

'Courier, one thousand metres!' he yelled jubilantly. 'We've got him, Dorfmann. We've got the bastard!'

The range closed rapidly, and now the other aircraft was easily identifiable as a four-engined heavy bomber with twin fins—either a Lancaster or a Halifax. Stechel didn't care which. The enemy aircraft cruised serenely on, its crew apparently unaware of the danger creeping up on them, and Stechel manœuvred his fighter carefully into position below and astern.

Something fell from the bomber's belly, almost causing him to break off in alarm, and for a second he watched the dark bundles as they curved down past his port wingtip. Then they came apart, breaking up into confetti-like showers of more of the strange metallic stuff that had almost given him heart failure thirty seconds easlier.

The bomber was huge in his sights now but still he held his fire, closing right in until he was less than a hundred metres astern and just a touch below. The enemy rear gunner must be asleep.

Taking infinite pains, Stechel raised the nose a fraction and sighted on the bomber's starboard wing between the two engines, a vulnerable spot where the fuel tanks were located. He could not understand why the Tommies had not equipped their bombers with ventral gun turrets as the Americans had done, so eliminating this dangerous blind spot.

He had selected cannon only and now his index fingers squeezed the twin triggers. A mixture of 30- and 20-mm cannon shells blasted out from the 110's nose guns, shaking the aircraft with the recoil and momentarily blinding the pilot with the muzzle flashes. Powder smoke drifted through the cockpit.

Belatedly, the bomber's rear gunner opened up, spraying tracer aimlessly into the night as Stechel's two-second burst slammed home. He dived steeply away from his target, ready to pull up for another attack, and saw at once that there would be no need. A dull red glow in the bomber's wing burst into a great streamer of fire, illuminating the square-cut tail fins; the target was now positively identified as a Halifax.

The ponderous bomber entered a diving turn to port, corkscrewing away from its attacker, its starboard wing now a mass of flame. Turning, Stechel followed it down as far as the cloud layer, watching it plunge into the opaque grey undercast. An instant later, a vivid orange flash split the clouds, followed in quick succession by several more of lesser intensity.

'Not much doubt about that one, sir,' commented Dorfmann, as the pilot regained altitude to resume his patrol. Nevertheless, it was the only enemy aircraft they saw that night, and they were luckier than most.

By the time the embers of Stechel's Halifax scattered themselves to extinction in the sea, some semblance of order was beginning to emerge from the chaos which had reigned in the operations room at Stade. Thirty minutes after midnight came the first reports that the leading elements of the bomber stream had turned south-east, and ten minutes later the crew of a night fighter called in to say that they had sighted bursts of yellow light, probably marker flares, over the mouth of the Elbe.

Richter glanced to his right and met the eyes of his neighbour, a tall captain who had spent the last two years on the Russian front and who wore the ribbon of the Knight's Cross. The man's face was grim. There was no longer any doubt about the RAF's target for tonight.

'It's Hamburg,' Richter said quietly. The other nodded. A few moments later, ground observers reported that the bombers were passing over Meldorf on a heading of approximately 110 degrees 'in great strength'. General Schwabedissen immediately ordered all night fighters within range to break away from their designated control sectors and converge on the city, but by the time they arrived it was too late.

The martyrdom of Hamburg began at exactly 0057 hours in the morning of 25 July 1943, when twenty aircraft of the RAF's Pathfinder Force dropped clusters of flares and target markers over the centre of the city. They were followed, five minutes later, by fifty-nine more bombers, each carrying a mixed load of incendiary markers and high explosive, so that by 0110 the area around the centre of Hamburg was lit up like a Christmas tree.

During the next forty minutes, 728 heavy bombers unloaded 2,400 tons of bombs on the hapless city, many of them incendiaries. Raging fires swept through the shattered streets, joining with one another to cause a great firestorm, fed by hurricane-force winds sucked in from Hamburg's perimeter. The winds picked up everything in their path, including people, and hurled it into the midst of the growing conflagration. Hundreds died in their air-raid shelters, suffocated by oxygen starvation as the inferno raged about them, their bodies reduced to ashes. Those who tried to flee were pulverized by high-explosive bombs, or mown down by flying débris. By 0145 a great sea of fire extended for seven miles between the docks area of Hamburg and the north-west suburbs.

Some bombs fell wide of the aiming point. One stick, jettisoned by a flak-damaged Lancaster, whistled down over the western suburbs and impacted on a maternity hospital. They killed sixty-seven people, mostly women and children. Among them were the wife and unborn child of Captain Wolfgang Lutz, who was trapped under a mound of rubble and eventually dug out, almost insane, nearly two days later.

To the personnel in the underground operations room of 2nd Air Division, the horror of Hamburg was something remote and impersonal. They had an inkling of it only through the terse reports that filtered in from the night fighters, groping blindly in the dark, from the flak batteries, the ground observers and the civil defence, and from the occasional tremor that shook the ground.

The radar was still useless, and not for some hours yet would the defenders know why. Throughout the raid, each bomber had dropped mysterious bundles—like those Stechel and Dorfmann had seen—at the rate of one every minute. The bundles broke apart and released thousands of strips of tinfoil, cut to the wavelengths of the German radar frequencies. Each strip produced a radar echo similar to that of an aircraft, jamming the radar screens with a mass of incomprehensible clutter. The British code-name for this simple and devastatingly effective device was 'Window'.

The last of the raiders droned away, and in the operations room the staff began to sift through the reports that had come in from the air defences. They held a grim portent for the future. Out of the vast armada that had smashed Hamburg, the flak and night fighters had shot down only twelve bombers.

The sun rose blood-red through the fires of the torn city. At dawn, an old man and his wife, haggard and red-eyed through lack of sleep and fear, emerged from the cellar of their little house on the outskirts of Stade and looked to the east.

Beyond the Elbe a massive pillar of smoke rose thousands of feet into the morning sky. It boiled and writhed, shot through with twisting ropes of black and brown. Its top spread out and drifted on the breeze, forming a dark, impenetrable carpet over their heads. They recoiled from it in terror.

17

'The chickens are coming home to roost,' muttered the old man, dragging himself on unwilling feet towards the stable at the bottom of the yard to tend to his mare.

Behind him, his wife whispered hoarsely: 'It is the will of God. The will of—'

Her voice broke in a sob and he turned towards her. She was leaning against the wall of their home, both hands clutched to her chest. He managed to catch her as she fell, and she died in his arms a few seconds later.

He carried her indoors and laid her gently on the sofa, closing her eyes. Then he went to the stable and stood for a long time, stroking the neck of his mare, soothing away the fear of the night. Deep within him, anguish was tearing him apart; but he had forgotten how to cry.

Chapter Two

THE TWO MEN WALKED ALONG THE NARROW LANE, THEIR shoes kicking up spurts of dust. All around them, apart from an occasional clump of trees and a distant church steeple, showing dimly through the low-lying wraiths of mist that were beginning to creep across the fens, the countryside was entirely flat. Away to the left, the sun was a vast red ball on the western horizon.

The men walked in silence, conscious of the evening sounds: the lowing of cattle, far away, the chatter of a startled blackbird, the rustle of unseen creatures in the hedgerow bordering the lane. Suddenly, one of the men, a grizzled warrant officer with two rows of medal ribbons indicating service in just about every part of the British Empire since the end of World War I, slowed his stride and turned to his companion, a much younger Flight Sergeant.

'Hang on, Sam,' the older man said. 'I'm not as young as I was. Let's stop for a smoke.'

The other nodded his assent and they perched on a nearby fence, unbuttoning their battledress and looking out over the quiet landscape. The warrant officer produced a crumpled packet of Player's and offered a cigarette to the flight sergeant before taking one himself. They both lit up, the smoke smelling sweet in the open air.

The flight sergeant belched suddenly and the man beside him grinned.

'Station farm, duty pig speaking,' he said.

'It's that bloody beer, Len,' the other protested. 'Can't get away with it at all. Don't tell me the locals have been drinking the stuff for years—I saw the look in their eyes as we were leaving. I'll bet the landlord got some real stuff out as soon as the door closed behind us.'

Warrant Officer Len Thomas made no reply. Personally, he liked the little tavern on the village green, even though most of the other senior NCOs from RAF Burningham went elsewhere and it was a four-mile walk from the airfield. Then he smiled inwardly, admitting to himself that what he really liked about the place was the landlord's sister, Betty, a plump rosy-cheeked widow in her forties whose husband had been killed in North Africa. Maybe, he thought, when she'd had time to forget, and things had settled down a bit, he'd ask her if she would consider getting together with him. A man might do a lot worse.

Thomas took a pull at his cigarette and then looked down at his hands, spreading out his fingers. They were broad and muscular and he was suddenly, for the first time in his life, acutely ashamed of them, of the ingrained oil and dirt collected in years of grovelling around in the guts of aeroengines. It seemed that no amount of scrubbing would remove it, but he resolved to try harder. That sort of thing might put a woman off for good.

'They're early tonight,' said Sam Porter, the flight sergeant, his voice cutting abruptly across Thomas's thoughts.

'What?'

Porter jerked a thumb towards the south-east and Thomas stared out across the fens, over the pools of mist, puzzled for a moment. Then he, too, heard the unmistakable note of engines, muted at first, then swelling gradually to a full-throated roar. Both men stood up, scanning the horizon, but as yet no aircraft was visible.

'There he is,' Porter said, pointing. Thomas saw it at the same instant: a long, dark shape, rising above the mist several miles away, but nevertheless recognizable as a Short Stirling bomber by its tall tailfin. The Stirling turned and climbed steadily away towards the east; it was followed by another and another. The two men counted fifteen in all, following each one as it climbed out over East Anglia until it was lost in the gathering gloom, heading for a rendezvous point with hundreds of others from airfields all over eastern England. The sky over the coast near Great Yarmouth would soon be echoing with man-made thunder as the great bombers wheeled like a flock of rooks before sorting themselves out into their designated stations and heading into the eastern darkness towards their distant target.

'I wonder if it's Hamburg again,' said Thomas.

'Doubt it,' Porter retorted. 'They've hit Hamburg three times this week already. They'll be off to somewhere in the Ruhr, more likely. I don't fancy their job, poor buggers. Especially in Stirlings. The bloody things won't climb above fifteen thousand.'

Porter frowned suddenly and threw his cigarette end into the road. 'Still,' he went on, 'at least they're operational. I'm beginning to think our lot will never get into action. I nearly had a fight with a bomber boy in Downham Market the other day; "the no-op squadron", he called us. But he was dead right.'

Thomas looked at him sharply. 'Don't you worry,' he said. 'The CO knows what he's doing. He won't declare the squadron fully operational until every man knows his job inside out, and that includes engine fitters, my son. Working up a new squadron is never easy; I've seen it all before. It takes time to build up a team, but this is going to be a good one, I can feel it in my bones. Those lads can fly, and the CO's the best of the lot.'

There was a note of pride in his voice. Porter sniffed and began to fasten up his battledress buttons, for a sudden chill had crept into the air as the sun sank below the horizon.

'You knew him before, didn't you.' It was a statement, rather than a question.

Thomas smiled and nodded. 'Aye, I did,' he said, his voice betraying his Lancashire origins. 'In France, before Dunkirk. Green as grass, he was, but he soon learned. He

21

was luckier than most. Got shot down, hitch-hiked his way across half France, got shot down again and came off the beaches with the army. Went through the fighting in August and September '40, too.'

'Seems a bit funny though, having a single-seat fighter bloke commanding a Mosquito squadron,' Porter said.

Thomas removed his forage cap and scratched his head. 'Oh, I don't know. He's got a hell of a lot of experience. He was in North Africa and Malta too, you know. And I heard on the grapevine that he didn't volunteer for a transfer to twin-engined aircraft; he was sent on the Mossie conversion course, got in a few ops with 2 Group and then they promoted him and told him to get on with the job of forming a squadron.'

Porter looked sideways at his friend. 'You seem to know a lot about it,' he said.

Thomas grinned. 'Comes of having mates in admin., if you want to know the secret.' He put on his cap again and shivered slightly.

'Damn it, it's turning cold. Come on, let's get a move on. It's not for the likes of you and me, Sam, to question who gets posted where or why. Our job's to keep the Merlins turning.'

He glanced at his watch. 'There's just time for one in the Mess, and then we'd better turn in. The squadron will be back first thing in the morning, and no doubt there'll be the usual number of snags to sort out. I hate the very thought of other people tampering with my lovely engines.'

Porter laughed. 'You've just got to remember that there's a war on,' he said. Together, they walked off in the rapidly spreading dusk.

Squadron Leader George Yeoman, DFC, DFM, was nursing a hangover. He felt for his oxygen mask, which was dangling loose by its strap, clipped it into position over his face, turned the oxygen fully on and took several deep breaths. His head began to clear almost at once, but in his stomach the breakfast he had forced down was only just holding its own with the residue of last night's alcohol.

It was six o'clock in the morning of 1 August 1943, and the ten Mosquitos of No. 380 Squadron, RAF, were returning to their Norfolk airfield of Burningham after spending four days at the Armament Practice Camp at Fairwood Common, in Gloucestershire. It had been a hectic period during which No. 380's crews had flown intensively, carrying out air-to-air firing against towed targets, live bombing exercises off the Welsh coast, and practice interceptions on the Beaufighters of No. 68 Squadron, which shared Fairwood Common with the APC.

Yeoman made a mental resolution never, ever, to drink again with 68 Squadron. He hadn't intended things to get out of hand, but a spontaneous party had developed because 380's last night at Fairwood Common had just happened to coincide with the award of a DFC to one of the 68 Squadron navigators.

Still, he thought, his chaps had deserved to let their hair down. He had been driving them pretty hard over the last few weeks, and now they were as good as he could make them. The squadron was a team at last, right down to the lowliest airman.

'Not feeling very well, skipper?'

Yeoman glanced over his right shoulder into the mournful features of his navigator, Flying Officer Steve Hardy, who was known as 'Happy' Hardy because he had never been known to smile. He had a remarkable capacity for beer though, and he had been known to do outrageous things to unsuspecting people. There had been the time on his previous squadron, for instance, when he had released two large, angry and very malodorous billy-goats into the ante-room of the officers' mess, which at the time had been full of Very Important Visitors and their Equally Important Wives. The story was legendary, and Yeoman wondered how Hardy had escaped without being hanged, drawn and quartered. Perhaps the fact that he was one of the best navigators in the Air Force had something to do with it.

Hardy was sporting a black eye this morning, the result of violent contact with someone's elbow during a game of Mess Rugby with the 68 Squadron types. It made him look even more like a sick spaniel.

'How do I look?' Yeoman asked.

'Bloody awful. How about me?'

'Worse. How long to base?'

'Ten minutes. If you'll stop wandering all over the sky, that is. Left two degrees.'

He looked back, twisting in his seat harness. 'The others are following you like a lot of lemmings. Straggling all over the place. I don't think we've got one good brain between us.'

Yeoman grunted. 'I think you're right. And I've no doubt the Station Commander will be there to meet us when we get back. Better get this lot sorted out.'

He pressed the R/T button. 'Squirrel Leader to Squirrel Aircraft. Close up.'

His words had the desired effect. A second Mosquito nosed its way into position beyond and behind his starboard wing, followed by two others, while a fourth aircraft placed itself off to the left. Within the space of half a minute the formation had arranged itself into two compact flights of four aircraft, with the two remaining Mosquitos bringing up the rear. Yeoman smiled to himself, satisfied, knowing that his pilots had reacted instinctively to his order.

The Mosquitos cruised on at a steady 230 mph, five thousand feet above the tranquil English countryside, their Rolls-Royce Merlin 21 engines singing healthily. Yeoman relaxed, feeling better now, allowing his hand to rest gently on the control column, his gaze automatically roving across the instrument panel, then to the sky and the aircraft around him, then back to the panel again.

It was funny, thought Yeoman, how he had got used to the idea of carrying a navigator, even after more than three years of flying single-seat fighters. Hardy had become almost an extension of himself, like an extra limb in the cockpit, an unobtrusive voice over the intercom, shepherding, guiding, sometimes admonishing, always striving for perfection. And that was how it ought to be; it was the recipe for survival.

The morning was brilliant, the sky cloudless, the sun burning the eyeballs even through smoked glasses, its rays dancing on cockpit canopies and the shimmering arcs of the propellers.

Somehow, it made the outlines of the Mosquitos, with their drab war-paint—dark grey and green upper surfaces, grey bellies—appear less aggressive.

Yet aggressive the Mosquito Mk VI certainly was, and powerful too, but nonetheless clean and graceful; an inspiration both to look at and to fly. Yeoman, who at first had viewed his conversion to twin-engined aircraft with considerable misgivings, had fallen completely in love with it. Its revolutionary concept appealed to him, for a start. Conceived as an unarmed day bomber back in 1938 by the de Havilland Aircraft Company, without any government approval or funding whatsoever, it was built from balsawood ply and birch laths, glued under pressure, a process that endowed it with a remarkable lightness as well as great strength, and its twin Rolls-Royce Merlin engines gave it a speed that compared favourably with most single-engined fighters of the day. It was fully aerobatic, too, and could be rolled on one engine.

The Mosquito FB Mk VI was the latest variant, and the newly-formed No. 380 Squadron had been one of the first to equip with the type, receiving its first examples in May 1943. Formidably armed with a battery of four 20-mm cannon and four .303 machine-guns in the nose, the Mk VI could also carry two 250- or 500-lb bombs in the rear of the bomb-bay, with two additional bombs or 50-gallon fuel tanks under the wings.

Mosquitos had been taking the war to the enemy ever since the end of March 1942, when No. 105 Squadron, flying the unarmed bomber version, had attacked Cologne the day after the RAF's first big thousand-bomber raid. More spectacular missions had followed, including a daring low-level raid on the Gestapo HQ in Oslo on 25 September and an attack on Berlin by Nos. 105 and 139 Squadrons, the first time RAF aircraft had flown over the enemy capital in daylight. That raid had been brilliantly timed to coincide with the tenth anniversary celebrations of the Nazi Party; all over Germany, people had been sitting by their radios, waiting to hear a speech by Reichsmarschall Hermann Goering. Instead, they had heard the sound of the Mosquitos' bombs, exploding near the radio station in Berlin.

Looking over to his left, Yeoman saw an airfield, with the dark shapes of Stirlings visible on their dispersal points even through the early morning haze. That was RAF Mepal, the home of No. 75 (New Zealand) Squadron. The Mosquitos were nearly home; the town of Ely lay dead ahead, with Burningham not far beyond it.

Yeoman called up Burningham Tower and obtained immediate clearance to land, leading the formation down in a descent to two thousand feet. The Mosquitos drummed over the airfield and then broke into line astern, joining the downwind leg of the circuit. Yeoman carried out his landing checks: brake pressure and superchargers okay, radiator flaps open, under-carriage down. He heard the landing gear lock into position with a thump, saw the reassuring green lights on his indicator. Reaching down with his left hand to the throttle quadrant, he pushed the propeller speed control fully forward, then switched the fuel cock to the fullest tanks.

A check with the yellow windsock showed him that there wasn't much wind, so he lowered full flap just before he turned on to final approach, trimming the aircraft nose-down to compensate and reducing the speed to 125 mph as he lined up with the runway. A few seconds later the Mosquito's wheels kissed the tarmac with a barely perceptible tremor.

'One of your better ones, skipper,' Hardy complimented him.

'They always are, on the morning after a binge,' the pilot replied. 'I have the fragility of my head to think about.'

Yeoman taxied in, bringing the Mosquito to a stop at its dispersal and shutting down the engines. He turned off the fuel, ignition and electrical masterswitch, then unfastened his harness and pulled off his helmet, easing himself out of his seat. Hardy opened the small hatch in the cockpit side and dropped the short ladder. The two men clambered down, gratefully inhaling the morning air, and nodded to the waiting ground crew. Yeoman exchanged a few words with the corporal in charge, then turned to watch the other Mosquitos as they taxied in.

A Humber staff car came round the perimeter track, heading towards them.

'Here comes the reception committee,' Hardy said. 'I told you the CO would be watching.'

Yeoman peered at the approaching vehicle, shading his eyes against the low-angle sun. 'It's the CO's car all right,' he muttered, 'but there doesn't seem to be anyone in it except the driver. And unless my eyes deceive me, it's little Saunders.'

'Could be your lucky day, skipper,' said Hardy. Senior Aircraftwoman Joan Saunders, the Group Captain's driver, was one of the most highly desirable inhabitants of RAF Burningham. She was also, by all accounts, the least attainable.

The Humber stopped and SACW Saunders got out, straightening her cap. She walked smartly across the grass towards Yeoman and Hardy, her hips swinging, every inch a woman despite the somewhat unbecoming uniform.

'Grrr,' said Hardy, so that only Yeoman could hear him. 'That's worth a court martial, any day.'

'Good morning, sir,' Saunders said, saluting and addressing Yeoman. 'The Group Captain sends his compliments, sir, and would like to see you in his office.'

'Very well,' Yeoman said. 'Thank you.' WAAFS always made him feel uncomfortable; it didn't seem right to address a pretty young girl by her surname. He turned to Hardy, who was gazing glassy-eyed at a point midway between Saunders' top two tunic buttons, and dumped his parachute into the arms of the navigator, who was already burdened with his own.

'Look after that for me, Happy,' he grinned. 'The walk over to the crew room will do you good.'

'Oh, thank you, skipper,' said Hardy sarcastically. 'Thank you very much indeed.'

In the car, Yeoman unfastened the small bag containing the personal belongings he had taken with him to Fairwood Common and took out his cap. It was his second best, much the worse for wear, with a large oil stain across the peak, and he was very much attached to it, for it had been with him throughout his hectic time in Malta. He put it on and then, reaching down, pulled his trouser-bottoms free of his flying-boots, trying in vain to smooth out the creases.

'Do I have time to get changed before I visit the station commander?' he asked Saunders, as they drove off past the hangars.

'Well, sir, he told me to bring you over as soon as you landed. There's another officer with him, sir, from Group HQ, and I think he's anxious to get away as soon as he's had a word with you. So his driver said, anyhow.'

The Humber deposited Yeoman at the main entrance to station headquarters, which consisted of a series of Nissen huts joined together to form a single complex housing all the administrative paraphernalia essential to the smooth running of a RAF station. Yeoman walked along a corridor, turned a corner and ran headlong into the adjutant, Flight Lieutenant Rees, an elderly, wisp-like man with an enormous moustache and wizened, sun-dried features. He had served in Mesopotamia during the 1914–18 War, and in Egypt and India for years afterwards.

Rees dropped a sheaf of papers on the floor and the pilot stooped to help him pick them up.

'Sorry, Adj.,' he apologized. 'I'm in a bit of a hurry; the CO wants to see me.'

'That's all right,' Rees said. 'It's nice to see you back. As a matter of fact, I was just going to have a peek outside to see if there was any sign of you.'

'What's going on?' Yeoman wanted to know, full of curiosity.

'Haven't a clue, old boy. There's one sure way to find out, though.'

Rees beckoned and led the way to his office, which adjoined the station commander's at the end of the corridor. It was shared by the adjutant, a redoubtable flight sergeant through whose scrutiny all visitors had to pass and a little WAAF filing clerk who made endless cups of tea. The flight sergeant rose as Yeoman walked in behind Rees, bade him a curt 'Good morning, sir,' his glance taking in the pilot's greasy hat and crumpled trousers, and then subsided again behind a mound of paperwork. Followed by Yeoman, Rees crossed his office and tapped on a door at the far side marked 'Officer Commanding'. He opened it, stuck his head inside

28

to announce the pilot's arrival, then stood aside to allow Yeoman to enter.

Group Captain Hector Davison, DSO, MC, looked sharply over the top of his half-moon glasses at Yeoman as the latter came into the office and saluted. Despite his quiet, school-masterish appearance, the medal ribbons which the commanding officer of RAF Burningham wore below the pilot's brevet on his tunic testified to his experience, and the cold, piercing blue eyes clearly brooked no inefficiency. He wasted no time on preliminaries, but waved a hand in the direction of a second senior officer who was standing by the window, sipping tea.

'Yeoman,' he said, 'this is Group Captain Sampson from the Directorate of Operations, Air Ministry. He wants to talk to you. Sit down and smoke if you like.'

'Thank you, sir.' Yeoman crossed the room, shook hands with Sampson and sat down in one of the leather armchairs facing Davison's desk. He searched his pockets for his pipe, then remembered that he had left it in his bag which was still in the outer office.

'Well, Yeoman,' said Sampson, setting down his cup and saucer on the window-sill, 'how are your chaps shaping up?'

'Pretty well, sir. I'll need to keep an eye on the odd one for a while, but they're a good bunch. Keen as mustard to start operations.'

Sampson nodded, thoughtfully stroking his chin with an index finger, and in the pause before he spoke again Yeoman took the opportunity to study him carefully. He realized with a start that, despite a swathe of grey hair that gave the group captain a badger-like appearance, Sampson was probably not yet forty years old; and then, as the man half-turned and the light from the window fell on his medal ribbons, Yeoman remembered.

It had been in March 1941, and Sampson had led nine Blenheims in a gallant, suicidal attack on a group of German warships off Wilhelmshaven. The flak had been murderous and the fighters had been waiting, and one Blenheim after another had gone down in flames, but Sampson had brought the survivors through a storm of fire and got them home, riddled with holes and at low level all the way. That was why, on the breast of his tunic, he wore the mauve ribbon of the Victoria Cross.

'Have you ever wondered why you were picked to form a Mosquito squadron, Yeoman?' Sampson asked suddenly.

'Yes, sir, I have,' the pilot admitted. 'But I'm glad it happened. The Mossie is a very fine aeroplane, and I wouldn't have missed it for the world.' He grinned. 'Almost like a Spitfire with twin engines, you might say.'

Sampson smiled. 'That's right, and it leads me nicely in to the point of this conversation, because there's one thing the Mosquito possesses which a Spitfire doesn't have, and that is range. Its armament is also excellent, and it has two attributes normally associated with single-seat fighters: speed and manœuvrability. All of which adds up to an ideal aircraft for fast, long-range operations against the enemy.'

Yeoman remained silent, wondering what was coming next. Surely, he thought, Sampson had not come all the way to Burningham to tell him something he knew already.

'No. 380 Squadron,' the group captain continued, 'was originally formed as part of No. 2 Group's striking force, for the purpose of carrying out low-level attacks, mainly by day, on specific objectives on the continent of Europe. As you are aware, there are already eleven other squadrons within the Group, each with more or less the same task. They will eventually form the spearhead of a greatly expanded and powerful tactical force which will operate in direct support of Allied land forces when the day comes to push back across the Channel.'

Yeoman pricked up his ears. It was the first time he had heard anyone in authority mention a forthcoming Allied invasion of Europe in such definite terms.

'However,' Sampson went on, 'your squadron will not be operating in the tactical role, although for reasons of security that is the impression we have fostered so far, and will continue to foster for as long as possible. Let me explain further.'

He reached out and picked up a pink folder from the edge of Davidson's desk. He tapped it with his index finger and said: 'This is our profit and loss account, Yeoman. A summary of the operations of RAF Bomber Command and the United States Eighth Bomber Command since March this year, since we stepped up the scope of our attacks on industrial targets in Germany.'

Sampson leafed through the folder, then closed it and laid it aside. He obviously knew its contents by heart.

'The statistics are interesting,' he said, 'and somewhat alarming. Our own night offensive against the Ruhr began well enough; when we attacked Essen on 5 March with 350 aircraft, for example, fourteen of our bombers failed to return, which was quite an acceptable percentage, and when we went to Nuremberg with three hundred bombers three nights later the loss was down to seven. These results, we thought, were very encouraging.

'Then we returned to Essen with four hundred bombers on 12 March, and this time we lost twenty-three, with a further sixty-nine damaged. We lost a further twenty-one against the same objective in April. In fact, during five attacks on Essen up to the end of May, our losses were ninety-two heavy bombers, with a further 334 damaged.'

Sampson's voice was dry and dispassionate, but there was an expression in the group captain's eyes the younger pilot knew only too well. The loss of ninety-two heavy bombers also meant the loss of over six hundred aircrew. Add that to the losses sustained during other attacks over the same period, and you had a tragedy.

Sampson tapped the folder again, then went on: 'This summary ends with the first big attack on Hamburg a few nights ago, when, thanks to the use of a new countermeasures device—bundles of metal foil, which proved very effective in jamming enemy radar—our losses fell to twelve aircraft out of a total force of 790. In a second attack on Hamburg, with a similar number of bombers, the loss was seventeen— still far within acceptable limits. We felt that the introduction of the new countermeasures was timely, because Bomber Command's total losses between the beginning of April and the middle of July were nearly nine hundred aircraft.'

'Good God!' The exclamation burst from Yeoman involuntarily. Nine hundred aircraft: more than six thousand young men, not counting the dead and injured in bombers that did manage to get home.

Sampson noted his reaction. 'Yes,' he said, 'it's pretty grim isn't it?'

'It's bloody well criminal!' snapped Davison, who so far had been following Sampson's comments in silence. 'I know for a fact that we've had this tinfoil thing up our sleeves for months, but have been too scared to use it in case the Germans cottoned on to the idea and used it back at us. We might have saved hundreds of lives.'

'Well, Hector, these things happen,' Sampson pointed out. 'Anyway, it's not for us to criticize. No doubt the decision seemed right at the time.' There was mild reproof in his tone; Davison grunted and sat back in his chair, glowering over the top of his spectacles.

'In any case,' Sampson continued, 'our troubles are by no means over, because thirty aircraft failed to return from the third raid on Hamburg, and first indications are that losses were also high during last night's attack, although we won't know precise details for some hours yet. If they are high, though—say thirty aircraft or more—it may indicate that our countermeasures are beginning to lose some of their effectiveness, or that the enemy night fighters have adopted new tactics, or both.'

He paused and cleared his throat, glancing out of the window as a motor cycle went by noisily, then turned back to Yeoman.

'If that is so,' he went on, 'the consequences may be very serious indeed. The present joint Anglo-American strategic bombing offensive is vital to the success of any future invasion of enemy-held territory, yet we cannot continue to suffer prohibitive losses. The Americans are being hurt badly, too, in their daylight operations over Germany; in one week last month they lost eighty-eight aircraft.'

'Never did agree with daylight operations,' muttered Davison. 'Sheer bloody suicide.'

'I couldn't agree more, Hector,' said Sampson wryly, and Davison flushed in sudden embarrassment.

'Sorry, old boy,' he said gruffly. 'I forgot you know more about daylight bomber ops than most of us.'

'Well,' Sampson went on, 'the point is the Americans think they can get away with it, and with strong fighter escort they probably can. Unfortunately, no fighter exists that can escort them all the way to the target and back, although there's talk of one coming along in a few months' time; meanwhile, their Thunderbolts and Lightnings can escort the bombers as far as the German border and our Spitfires can meet them on the way home, but that's about all we can do.'

Oh, my God, thought Yeoman, he's going to suggest that we use our Mosquitos as escort fighters.

He was wrong, and his eyes must have betrayed his thoughts, because Sampson smiled faintly and said: 'Don't worry, Yeoman, we're not going to ask you to fly top cover for the Fortresses all the way to Berlin and back. Your task will be to provide bomber support of a different kind.'

He shifted his position and moved forward a few steps, standing with his hands clasped behind his back and looking down at the younger man.

'Within the next few days,' hs said, 'No. 380 will be joined here at Burningham by a second Mosquito squadron. It has recently converted from Beaufighters and is now operating modified Mk VIS, equipped with the latest airborne interception radar.

'Although still technically under the control of No. 2 Group, the two squadrons of the Burningham Wing will have a considerable degree of autonomy and will operate as intruders by day and night, ranging deep into enemy territory. Their targets, above all, will be the German Fighter Command and its principal airfields.'

The group captain looked long and hard at Yeoman, and was inwardly pleased by the enthusiasm which the pilot made no attempt to hide.

'It will be dangerous and exacting work,' he continued, 'and now perhaps you have an inkling of why you were chosen for this job. We needed someone with a thorough knowledge of German fighter procedures and tactics; someone who had fought the enemy in every theatre. That someone was you. For the time being, you will be in overall command of the Wing.

'I may as well tell you that a new Group is soon to be

formed for the specific task of bomber support; that is to say intruder and countermeasures work against the enemy air defences. The Burningham Wing will pioneer the techniques which, we hope, will form the basis of a highly efficient and elite force—a force whose aim will be to confound and destroy.'

He stopped and looked at Group Captain Davison. 'You know, Hector,' he smiled, 'that could be quite a nice motto for the new Group. I must put up the idea to someone. Yes, the words have a fine ring. "Confound and Destroy".'

He turned back to Yeoman and said: 'Well, that's about it. Do you have any questions?'

Yeoman stood up, picking up his cap from the chair arm. 'Just one, sir,' he said. 'When do we start?'

Chapter Three

'WELL, SIR, HOW DOES IT FEEL TO BE BACK IN HARNESS?'

Joachim Richter lowered the magazine he had been reading and looked up, startled by the sudden question, from his chair in a corner of the flight hut. He removed his smoked glasses, which all pilots on readiness for night operations wore, and massaged his eyes carefully with the tips of his fingers. He'd been getting headaches lately, possibly caused by eyestrain. He ought to do something about that.

He smiled at the speaker, Lieutenant Johnny Schumacher, who had fought alongside him over Malta a year earlier. Although glad to be away from the operations room at Stade, Richter's posting to a completely strange unit instead of his old and familiar Fighter Wing 66 had come as a bitter disappointment, so it had been a welcome surprise when Schumacher had also turned up.

'It feels good, Johnny. Very good indeed. I know a lot of you types don't like this idea of flying single-engined fighters at night, but personally I don't give a damn. Just give me a Gustav and some cannon and I'll shoot Tommies off the moon, if I have to.'

Schumacher laughed. 'As bloodthirsty as ever! Seriously, though, do you think this scheme is going to work?'

The scheme to which he referred had been dreamed up a couple of weeks earlier by a Major Hajo Hermann, a Luft-

35

waffe lecturer in fighter tactics who was also a pilot of considerable repute. Lecturing during the day, as soon as evening arrived he would drive furiously to a nearby airfield and jump into the cockpit of a Focke-Wulf 190, which was specially fitted with a 400-litre auxiliary tank to extend its endurance to two and a half hours. When an alert sounded and the probable target of the RAF night bombers was known, he would take off and roam the sky looking for trouble at heights of up to 30,000 feet, far above the bomber stream. He reasoned that wherever searchlights and flak appeared there must also be enemy bombers, and although his Focke-Wulf had no radar aids at all Hermann used his sharp eyesight to pick out his targets, silhouetted in the glare of Germany's burning cities.

After a handful of pilots using the same tactics had shot down a dozen RAF heavy bombers during one of the raids on Hamburg, the Luftwaffe High Command had fallen in love with the idea and authorized night operations by single-engined day fighters on a large scale. The code-name for these operations was 'Wild Boar'.

Richter sighed and flexed his arms. In common with the other eight or nine pilots in the room, he was wearing full flying kit and he felt hot and uncomfortable. Nevertheless, he had just rebuked one young pilot for removing his flying-jacket; items of flying clothing could easily be mislaid in the commotion following an alert, and precious seconds wasted in searching for them.

'I don't know, Johnny,' he said, in response to Schumacher's question. 'All I do know is that anything is worth a try. The bombers aren't invincible, but we need more fighters.'

He lowered his voice a little, so that only Schumacher could hear. 'I've heard there's talk of turning a lot of our aircraft production over to building a new reprisal bomber, something so fast that the Tommies won't be able to catch it, and then there's all this talk about secret weapons. To my mind, it's all bloody nonsense. We've got to concentrate all our resources on shooting down so many Tommies and Amis that they'll think twice about venturing over the Fatherland in strength, by day or night.'

He got up suddenly. 'I'm off outside for a breath of fresh air,' he said. 'Are you coming?'

He made his way to the door, pausing to kick a stool from under the feet of a leather-jacketed pilot who was draped across an armchair, snoring gently. 'Wake up, Lodz, you lazy sod,' he snapped. 'Stick your head out of the door and yell if anything happens.'

He went outside, followed by Schumacher, and stood with his hands in his pockets, gazing moodily into the dusk. A short distance away, darkly aggressive and silent, stood the fighters, a mixed bag of fifteen Messerschmitt 109Gs and Focke-Wulf 190s, the latter ungainly on their long, stalky undercarriages. They comprised the equipment of No. 2 Squadron, Fighter Wing 301, which Richter now commanded. Six of them were unserviceable, despite the trojan efforts of the squadron's mechanics; they were patched-up, worn-out machines drawn from other units, and those units seemed to have been only too glad to get rid of them. Just a couple of hours earlier, Richter had been approached by Flight Sergeant Handke, the squadron's senior engine fitter, who had told him despairingly that three of the aircraft would never be fit to fly. God only knew, Handke had said, how they got here in the first place without falling apart.

Although he had only known Handke for a few days, Richter had sensed at once that he was a good and experienced NCO who knew what he was talking about, so he had ordered him to ground the three suspect fighters and use them for spare parts. Such a move really needed the signature of a senior technical officer, but there wasn't one, and anyway as far as Richter was concerned the proper channels could go to hell. Until replacement aircraft could be found, the cannibalized machines would help to keep the others airworthy.

'Any more news on when we can expect the other squadrons to move in, sir?' Schumacher asked. Two more 'Wild Boar' units had been scheduled to arrive at the airfield, a hastily-prepared strip a few miles from Munster, three days ago, but there had been a hold-up somewhere along the line. Richter shook his head.

'No, thank heaven. When they do arrive it will be absolute

37

chaos. Can you imagine it—a complete group operating out of this dump? Christ, they haven't even finished digging the latrines yet.'

Schumacher grinned. 'Yes, even Sicily was more civilized.' His face suddenly became serious. 'I'll bet it isn't now, though. That's one battle we seem to have lost. The Yanks and Tommies will be in Italy in no time.'

Richter looked at him sharply. 'Careful, Johnny. That would be called defeatist talk in most circles.' He drew his forefinger across his throat in a meaningful gesture. 'Still,' he went on, 'I know what you mean. I think, however, that our opponents will find Italy a tough nut to crack. I hope they get bogged down in those damned mountains forever, and have to divert all their bombers there.'

He peered at his watch, and then at the sky. There was a high overcast against which it would be relatively easy to spot enemy aircraft. 'If they come, that is,' he remarked absentmindedly. 'Well, we should know in another hour or so.'

He was right. Exactly seventy minutes later, the telephone in the flight hut—the direct line to Fighter Control—began its clamour and the pilots raced for their aircraft across the dew-heavy grass. Richter hurled himself into the cockpit and a mechanic did up his straps while he began the starting-up procedure. The big three-bladed propeller turned a few times and then the Daimler-Benz 605 engine burst into harsh life, causing the aircraft to throb with sudden vitality.

As he taxied towards the dimly-lit flarepath, Richter felt a sudden urge to sing. The Messerschmitt 109G-6 was the latest version of that famous fighter, and he was sitting behind more power than he had ever known. The DB-605D engine had a powerful supercharger and a methanol-water injection system which, when mixed with 100-octane fuel, boosted output to 1,800 hp. Flat out, the 'Gustav-Six' could do over 400 mph. It could also climb to nearly 42,000 feet, giving it plenty of room for manœuvre in combat against American day bombers that sometimes operated at heights of 30,000 feet and more. Messerschmitt's designers, by providing a longer tailwheel assembly and a slightly taller fin and rudder,

38

had also managed to eliminate a tendency to swing savagely on take-off—a failing in earlier models of the 109 that had brought many an experienced pilot to grief.

Above all, Richter liked the G-6's armament. There were two 20-mm cannon slung in underwing gondolas, two 13-mm machine-guns mounted in the nose—and, finally, firing through the centre of the airscrew spinner, a massive 30-mm Mk 108 cannon that could virtually tear the wing off a bomber with a single shell.

Richter pressed the radio transmit button on his control column and called up the airfield controller.

'Starling, this is Elbe One. Taking off.'

'Victor, Elbe One, when airborne change to Thrush on channel two.'

Richter acknowledged curtly and opened the throttle. A slight forward pressure on the stick brought the tail up as the Messerschmitt gathered speed. The lights of the flarepath streamed by in a continuous blur and then he was airborne, bringing up his undercarriage and climbing hard into the darkness. Behind him, invisibly, the other Messerschmitts and Focke-Wulfs followed.

Richter changed the frequency selector on his VHF radio to channel two and contacted the fighter controller, code-named 'Thrush' in this particular sector.

'Thrush, this is Elbe One. Do you have trade?'

The response came back instantly. 'Victor, Elbe One, couriers now in Gertrud-Gertrud, Roland three-seven, orbit Erika, altitude Hanni two-nine.'

The controller was telling Richter that enemy aircraft were crossing the coast near Emden at 22,000 feet, and that he was instructed to circle at 25,000 feet over a radio beacon ten miles south of Lingen. Doing a rapid bit of mental calculation, the pilot reasoned that unless they changed course in the next few minutes, the enemy must be heading for Essen or one of its neighbouring towns in the Ruhr Valley.

At 18,000 feet Richter popped up through the cloud layer and found himself under a clear, velvet sky, spangled with brilliant stars. The moon had set, but the starlight alone was sufficient to illuminate the clouds; they stretched beneath him like a continuous white blanket, with a small peak jutting up here and there like the tip of a hidden mountain.

Richter continued to climb, levelling out at 25,000 feet, homing towards the radio beacon by the steady pulse of dots and dashes in his headphones. The cloud crawled slowly beneath him; he had a strange sense of being suspended in time and space.

When the tone in his headphones became continuous, telling him that he was directly over the beacon, he brought the Messerschmitt round in a wide circle and radioed the fighter controller again, asking if there was any further information. He was told that the incoming aircraft were now in sector Gertrud-Lore, course one-nine-zero, holding their height of 22,000 feet.

Richter frowned. Unless the controller had made a mistake, the raiders had come a long way in the last few minutes. They must be doing close on 300 mph—much too fast for Lancasters or Halifaxes.

Suddenly, Richter knew with grim certainty what was happening. Calling up the fighter controller once more, he asked for an estimate of the size of the raid. The reply came back straightaway:

'Elbe One, this is Thrush. Am unable to comply. Radar is being jammed.'

Richter wasted no time. Switching to the common fighter frequency, to which the pilots remained tuned when not actually in contact with one or other of the control stations, he shouted:

'All aircraft, all aircraft, this is Elbe One. Watch out for Mosquitos. I repeat, watch out for Mosquitos!'

In God's name, he swore, why hadn't the controllers woken up to what was happening? The speed of the targets should have alerted them. Those bloody infernal Mosquitos! There would be no more than a dozen of them, dashing across the north German coast at widely-spaced intervals, dropping their tinfoil bundles and creating as much confusion as possible.

Shooting down a Mosquito was a rare achievement, even in daylight, and by night Richter knew that it would be virtually impossible, with no radar aids to guide him to a likely target. It took him only a split second to reach a decision. Pressing the transmit button again, he called:

'All Elbe aircraft, this is Elbe One. Return to base. I repeat, return to base.'

Swinging the Messerschmitt round fiercely, he pointed its nose down through the cloud and set course for the airfield. Visual navigation was not easy, for the blackout was complete and waterways showed up only faintly in the featureless dark, but when he judged that he was close to home he radioed the aerodrome controller and told him to light the flarepath. He picked it out moments later, a tiny cluster of pearls in the blackness ahead and slightly off to the left.

Richter touched down, followed by other fighters at short intervals, and taxied towards the flight hut, switching off his engine. Flight Sergeant Handke came running out and the pilot issued rapid orders, telling him to have the aircrafts' fuel tanks topped up immediately. Then Richter sprinted into the hut and rang the duty controller, cutting short the beginning of a protest about the squadron's early return to base.

'To hell with that! You've got fighters stooging around up there, chasing a few blasted Mosquitos. Damn it, man, can't you see what the Tommies are up to? There's an attack on the way in, and they've timed it so that most of our aircraft will be on the ground refuelling when they arrive. For God's sake, get somebody to recall them, now! Otherwise it'll be too late.'

For most of them, it was. During the next hour, several more Mosquitos sped over German territory keeping the defences in a state of constant alert. Richter, and one or two other enterprising squadron commanders, kept their units on the ground, but many more fighters took off in a fruitless search for the elusive British intruders.

When the heavy bombers finally did come, there were more than two hundred of them, and their target was the important railway marshalling yards at Hamm. The bombers crossed the Dutch coast near the island of Ameland and then made a long feint into Germany, penetrating deeply in the direction of Bielefeld before swinging south-westwards towards their real target.

Richter, who had held his fighters on the ground until the

very last moment and then once again assembled them over beacon 'Erica', made contact with the head of the bomber stream near the little town of Warendorf. It was pure luck that brought him to a target. Circling blindly into the darkness, a few thousand feet above the cloud layer, he suddenly sighted a broad pool of diffused light a few miles to the north and realized that he was looking at a cone of searchlights, shining on the cloud base. He headed for the spot at full throttle, and as he approached he saw flak start to come up, bursting in orange pricks of light just above the cloud. Then he saw something else: a dull red spot, crawling slowly across the sky a little to one side of the flak concentration.

Puzzled, he steered towards it, losing a few hundred feet of height until he was below the level of the curious object and skipping just above the cloud tops.

Whatever the thing was, he was overhauling it rapidly. It seemed to float towards him and he throttled back slightly. It appeared to be stationary now, which indicated that he was astern of it, and he kept pace with it for half a minute, striving to identify it.

Then, cursing himself for a fool, he realized in a flash what it was. He was looking at an aircraft, presumably an enemy bomber, with one engine on fire.

He opened the throttle again, narrowing the distance until he could see the dark shape of the other machine quite clearly. He saw, now, that the fire was in the fuselage, perhaps the bomb bay, and not an engine at all. It was a small conflagration, but it burned like a beacon in the night.

Closing in cautiously, keeping just below the other aircraft's altitude, he made a positive identification. Twin engines mounted on long, slender wings, a deep fuselage with a single fin and rudder—characteristic recognition features of the Vickers Wellington.

At 150 metres Richter opened fire with cannon only, aiming carefully for the bomber's port engine. He knew that the Wellington could take terrific punishment, and recalled the stories of fellow fighter pilots who had engaged this type of bomber in the early days of the war, when the British had sent Wellingtons to attack the north German ports in daylight. Wellingtons had been shot full of holes, their fuselages ripped and torn, and had still managed to get away. To make sure of a Wellington you had to shoot for the engines or the wings, where the vulnerable fuel tanks were housed.

Richter did not miss. The Messerschmitt shuddered with the recoil of its cannon and a series of bright flashes twinkled across the bomber's wing. It immediately began to go down in a diving turn to the left as the pilot desperately tried to reach the sheltering cloud, but Richter fired again and this time his shells tore into the Wellington's wing root. There was a vivid explosion and flames streamed back past the tail, lighting up the drab camouflage and the fuselage roundel, their glare reflected from the perspex of the rear gunner's position.

Richter followed the stricken bomber down through the cloud, locating it again without difficulty as it twisted down in a tight spiral, burning fiercely. Searchlights locked on to it for a few seconds and the pilot saw a solitary parachute snap open and shine brightly in their beams before being swallowed up in the darkness.

The sudden burst of light was blinding; it was like being suspended in the middle of a goldfish bowl, with powerful torches shining in from all sides. Richter hastily pulled down his darkened goggles and climbed back through the cloud; it would be minutes before his night vision was restored. Anyway, there was no point in following the Wellington's death throes; it was obviously finished.

He called up fighter control and was told that Hamm was under attack; other fighters had already reported combats over the town. Richter headed rapidly in that direction and dropped under the cloud once more; below him, the broad band of the River Lippe, which ran through the town from east to west, shone blood-red in the light of the fires already started by the British bombs.

Richter patrolled over and around Hamm for a further hour, searching in vain for another contact but, although he could see the flashes of exploding bombs from time to time, the aircraft that dropped them eluded him completely. In the end he gave up and returned to base as his fuel ran out, swearing with rage and frustration.

Most of the others were already back, including Johnny

Schumacher, who was kicking furniture around the flight hut in a fit of towering anger. Richter told him to calm down and asked him what was the matter.

'I had a bomber,' snarled Schumacher. 'I had the bastard cold! I set him on fire with my first burst, but his rear gunner put out some very accurate return fire and I had to break off the first attack. He was lit up like a Christmas tree, so I had no trouble locating him again, and I was just getting nicely into position a few hundred metres astern to have another go when some son of a bitch cut across my nose and shot him down!'

'Oh,' said Richter. 'Tough luck. Tell me, Johnny, did you identify the enemy aircraft?'

'Yes. It was a Wellington.'

'And did you identify the fighter that robbed you of your prize, so to speak?'

'No, I didn't,' Schumacher admitted, 'more's the pity, because I'd like to wring the pilot's neck!'

'That would be a great pity,' grinned Richter. 'The Luftwaffe is quite short of squadron commanders of my calibre.'

Schumacher gaped at him, realization beginning to dawn slowly. Richter nodded at him solemnly.

'Yes,' he said, 'I'm afraid so, Johnny. It was me. But honestly, I didn't see you, and in any case the Wellington was done for. I'm giving you the credit for it. I just helped it on its way to perdition, as it were.'

The part about the Wellington being finished before Richter attacked it was not strictly true, but if Schumacher had not already set it on fire it was unlikely that Richter would have ever seen it. It was only fair, therefore, that the victory should be attributed to Schumacher.

Altogether, the pilots of No. 2 Squadron, Fighter Wing 301, had destroyed four of the enemy bombers which had attacked Hamm. It was a good start to the newly-formed unit's operational career. However, thought Richter, something would have to be done to tighten up fighter co-ordination, and stronger measures would certainly have to be taken to deal with those blasted Mosquitos.

Later that morning, Richter drove into Hamm to visit a

survivor of the raid, who had parachuted from the crippled Wellington and who was in hospital with broken ankles. He was a sergeant air gunner, a boy of eighteen, who looked up white-faced and frightened as the Luftwaffe officer stood beside his bed. Richter made an attempt to talk with him, but the boy shook his head and maintained a tight-lipped silence. In the end, the pilot gave up and left.

Outside the door of the ward, he bumped into the nursing sister in charge. Her eyes were glazed with fatigue; it had been a long night.

'See that the boy is well treated, sister,' Richter instructed.

The nurse looked at him and made no reply. The hospital was heavy with the acrid stench of smoke from the railway yards and the streets around them, still burning from the night's attack. Civilian casualties had been heavy.

These fools, she thought, as she stared at Richter's retreating back. These young fools who make war in their aeroplanes and their tanks and their ships, and then shake hands with one another afterwards as though it were all some kind of monstrous game. And always, without exception, it was the civilians who suffered most of all.

Chapter Four

IT WAS AN HOUR BEFORE SUNRISE, AND THE AIR WAS CHILLY. The lone cyclist shivered as he pedalled along the narrow road that ran behind the darkened hangars and wished heartily that he was back in the warmth of his bed. Then, mentally, he chastised himself for being selfish; his task would be over in less than an hour, and there would be time for more sleep before breakfast.

He halted outside a long Nissen hut and dismounted, letting his bicycle fall on its side on the grass. He entered the building and strode purposefully along a corridor, his footsteps echoing. At the far end of the corridor, a red-and-white notice on a door warned: NO ADMITTANCE TO UNAUTHORIZED PERSONNEL.

He paused at the door, listening for a moment to the murmur of voices beyond it, striving hard to control the nervousness he always felt at this point. He could never understand why he felt nervous; after all, the men on the other side of the door were not very much older than the boys he had been teaching at college only three years earlier. Perhaps that was part of the reason: that they were young and he was middle-aged, forming yet another barrier behind the greatest of all; that they had wings on their breasts, and he had none. He could not deny that they treated him as an equal and with great friendliness; every one of them called him by his first name. But he could never really belong to their circle, for they faced death and he did not, and every time he faced them on occasions like this he was conscious that the orders he carried might mean the brutal execution of some or all of them.

Their jocularity, their nonchalance, had also made him nervous, once; but not any more. In his three years of RAF service (three years that had cost him his home and his wife, for she had never forgiven him for volunteering) he had learned to laugh and joke with them, not as an equal, but as a benevolent uncle. He had also learned not to become too involved, personally, with any of them. In the beginning, during his time with a heavy bomber squadron, he had often acted as a kind of father confessor to some of the young aircrew who had passed through his life, and in a school-masterish sort of way had become very attached to them. But he had seen too many empty places at the Mess tables, and the inward misery had been too great.

Taking a deep breath, he turned the handle and opened the door, stepping into the room beyond, blinking owlishly behind the thick lenses of his horn-rimmed spectacles. There were a dozen men in the room, seated astride chairs or lounging on trestle tables; all of them were pilots, for this was the ritual known as the captain's briefing. The navigators were elsewhere, undergoing their own briefing session, poring over their maps and charts. Later everyone would get together for a short main briefing, during which any last-minute points would be raised and the aircrews addressed by the station commander. It was a lengthy process, but it ensured that all relevant information was passed down the line and that every individual knew precisely what was expected of him.

The newcomer's entry into the briefing room was greeted by a chorus of yells.

'Hey, Freddie, what's the gen?'

'Another short run, I hope!'

'Yeah, that's right, Calais or somewhere nice like that.'

'Come on, Freddie, give us the gen. What's the target?'

Flight Lieutenant Freddie Barnes, No. 380 Squadron's Intelligence officer, smiled faintly and crossed the room to the big wall map of western Europe that dominated the raised platform. Taking a coloured, round-headed pin from his pocket, he stuck it precisely in the middle of the formidable anti-aircraft defences of Berlin.

For a moment there was complete silence, then a roar of derision went up.

'Sod off, Freddie! It's too early in the morning for that sort of joke. Let's have it straight—where are we really going?'

Barnes turned back to the map, removed the pin from Berlin and stuck in three more, all of them at locations in Holland close to the German border. Using lengths of red tape, wound around other strategically-placed pins, he traced the route the Mosquitos would take from Burningham to their objectives and back again. With considerable relief, the pilots saw that most of it was over the sea; the deepest penetration they would have to make into enemy territory was about seventy miles.

'What sort of targets are they, Freddie?' The speaker, who had a mild Scots accent, was a tall, lean flight lieutenant with thinning red hair. His name was Rory McManners, and he was one of 380 Squadron's flight commanders. The other, a dark-haired and much younger Londoner named Tim Sloane, sat next to him. Both men had already completed two tours of operations, one on Blenheims and the other on Beaufighters.

'Airfields,' Barnes said. 'They're all airfields.'

'*Merde!*' The French oath cut sharply across the room, and Barnes peered at its source, a swarthy man with jet-black hair parted severely down the middle and glittering coals of eyes. He wore the dark blue uniform, with gold rank braid, of the Free French Air Force. Lieutenant Yves Romilly had flown Blenheims in North Africa, and had several times seen his squadron decimated in airfield attacks. He closed his eyes, rested his chin on his hands, and said no more.

More questions were hurled at Barnes, who held up both hands.

'Now then, chaps,' he protested, 'you know I can't tell

48

you any more until the CO and the specialist officers arrive. You'll just have to be patient.'

'Oh, all right, Freddie,' said Sloane. 'However, I should point out to you, before anyone else comes in, that you are improperly dressed.'

Barnes, a fussy man when it came to appearance, instinctively felt to see if the knot in his tie and his tunic buttons were fastened properly. They were. Then, looking down, he flushed with sudden embarrassment. He had forgotten to remove his cycle clips.

'Never mind, Freddie,' Sloane grinned, 'it might have been worse. Your flies might have been undone.'

During the next five minutes, the pilots and Barnes were joined by the various specialists—the meteorological, engineering, armaments and air traffic control officers—all of whom would have something to say in the course of the briefing. Everyone took a seat, and an air of expectancy settled over the briefing room as the hands of the wall clock moved towards 0400. Barnes noted with some surprise that, on this occasion, everyone had arrived early; normally, two or three aircrew burst into the room at the very last moment, panting and out of breath.

A few seconds before four o'clock, the door opened again and Group Captain Davison entered the room, followed by Yeoman. Everyone stood up, then sat down with a scraping of chairs as the Group Captain motioned to them to do so. He himself took a seat behind the assembled pilots, where he would remain an inconspicuous onlooker until the main briefing.

Yeoman stepped up on to the platform, placed his hat on a table and then stood facing the assembly, his hands behind his back, surveying the pilots for a second or two while he marshalled his thoughts.

'Good morning, gentlemen. I am aware that you are all champing at the bit because of the lack of activity over the past few days.'

There were a few murmurs of assent. Since the squadron had carried out its first long-range operational mission early

49

in August, dropping 'Window' in support of a night attack on Hamm by Bomber Command, operations had been badly disrupted by the weather. A few sorties had been flown by single aircraft, but these had involved patrols over the Channel or very short forays into enemy territory, the Mosquitos dropping down through low cloud and drizzle to shoot up targets of opportunity. So far, there had been no losses.

'Well,' Yeoman continued, 'today is the one we've all been waiting for. This morning, we shall be carrying out our first big operation by daylight—an attack on three enemy fighter airfields in Holland.'

He picked up a billiard cue that served as a pointer and moved over to the wall map, indicating the target airfields one by one.

'The first of them, and the one closest to the coast, is Eelde, five miles due south of Groningen. This will be attacked by McManners, Reed, Romilly and Olafsson. Further south, about forty miles inland'—the pointer moved down the map—'is Hoogeveen, which will be attacked by Sloane, O'Grady, Keen and Lorrimer. It's a fairly small grass field, right on the north-east outskirts of the neighbouring town, so you'll have to be careful not to endanger any Dutch lives.'

The pointer moved still further down the map, stopping at the third pin which Barnes had inserted a few minutes earlier.

'This is Twenthe, near Hengelo, and it's the closest of the lot to the German border. I'll look after that one, together with Miller, Saint and Telfer. It's seventy miles inland.'

'Thanks, boss,' said a rueful voice from the audience. There was a ripple of laughter; the speaker was Pilot Officer Terry Saint, a slightly-built New Zealander who was one of the squadron's chief comedians. Yeoman grinned at him.

'All right, Terry, I've no doubt you'll be taking a spare pair of underpants with you. Now, before we get down to technicalities, let's have a word about what we are likely to expect. Over to you, Freddie.'

Barnes rose and cleared his throat self-consciously, consulting a report he held in his hand.

'The last reconnaissance of this area,' he said, 'was carried out yesterday afternoon by a PRU Spitfire, so it's as up to date as we can make it. The indications are, first of all, that there are now four squadrons of Messerschmitt 109s at Eelde, with two more at Hoogeveen, and that there are three squadrons of Focke-Wulf 190s at Twenthe. Now here's the flak situation.'

He pinned up three large target photographs, one for each airfield, and pointed out the known anti-aircraft emplacements. Hoogeveen seemed to be relatively poorly defended, but the perimeters of the other two airfields were stiff with quadruple 20-mm quick-firing cannon, and these would trouble the low-flying Mosquitos far more than the heavier-calibre 37-mm weapons sited here and there. Yeoman noted, too, that the Germans had sited light-calibre flak batteries along the approaches to the runways, to protect their aircraft as they were coming in to land.

Barnes went on to give more information about the opposition the Mosquitos were likely to expect, then Yeoman resumed his briefing.

'Our call-sign will be Spanner,' he said. 'My section will be Spanner Red, McManners' Spanner Blue, and Sloane's Spanner Green. We shall be taking off at five-minute intervals, starting at 0530: Spanner Red first, then Green, then Blue, and we shall set course independently. In this way, we should all arrive over our targets at about the same time.

'It will be low-level all the way, and we shall fly parallel with the Frisian Islands until we are abeam Rottumerplaat, when we shall turn in over the Dutch coast. Absolute radio silence is essential, I need hardly tell you. If anyone has a problem, he should waggle his wings and return to base, still at low level, and switch to D Frequency, but for Christ's sake don't use it unless you are in really serious trouble.'

In front of him, the pilots were busily scribbling down relevant information on scraps of paper or the backs of their hands. The room was beginning to fill with cigarette smoke.

'And remember this,' Yeoman continued, 'let's have no heroics. There'll be time for one run over the target, and no more. Try to begin your attack on the side of the airfield away from the hangars and installations, giving yourselves plenty of time to shoot up anything you see before dropping the two 500-pounders you'll be carrying among the buildings. I'll leave it to the individual section leaders to work out the finer points with their chaps once they've had a good look at the target photos, but I would recommend detouring slightly to the east in order to attack out of the sun, wherever possible.

'If you are attacked, don't stay to fight; open the taps and piss off as fast as you can out to sea.'

Yeoman concluded his briefing with more advice and information, then turned over the platform to the specialist officers. For once, the weather forecast was optimistic; there was mist over East Anglia, but it was expected to clear at about 0500 and there should be no complications on either the outward or return flights. Cloud over western Europe would be four-tenths cumulus at eight thousand feet, and was not expected to increase or lower until late afternoon.

Yeoman listened absently to the specialist briefings, since he already knew the details, and took the opportunity to observe the pilots covertly, noting their reactions. There was no sign of any apprehension on any of their faces, not even on that of Flying Officer O'Grady, the one pilot about whom Yeoman had harboured certain reservations. O'Grady was a shy, retiring man of twenty-three who came from Liverpool, and Yeoman had never seen him take part in any of the spontaneous mess parties that sprang up from time to time; walking and reading seemed to be his main pastimes. That was his affair, but nevertheless Yeoman liked to see his pilots involved with one another socially; he knew from experience that it made for better teamwork in the air. However, he could find no fault with O'Grady's operational record; he had come to Mosquitos after a tour of operations on Westland Whirlwinds—fast, superb and highly manœuvrable fighters cursed with twin Rolls-Royce Peregrine engines which had produced an incessant spate of troubles—and was the only pilot on the squadron who had flown long-range daylight escort missions over occupied Europe, before the RAF's two Whirlwind squadrons had gone over to ground attack.

Yeoman had the feeling that the root of O'Grady's problem—if, indeed, he had a problem—was that the man had some sort of chip on his shoulder. Something to do with his background, perhaps. Yet the majority of the men in the room came from relatively humble backgrounds; Yeoman's own father was a gamekeeper, which had absolutely nothing at all to do with Yeoman's own ability. Or maybe it had, for John Yeoman had taught his son the one thing essential in the making of a successful fighter pilot: the art of deflection shooting, and of hitting the target first time. Anyhow, Yeoman sensed that something deep down was bothering O'Grady, and he was determined to find out what it was.

Of the others, as far as he knew, only Pilot Officer Reed was a former public schoolboy, and it showed in his accent and mannerisms. Six feet tall and of athletic build, with corn-coloured wavy hair, his uniform was always immaculately tailored and pressed and he exuded self-confidence from every pore. He was the only first-tour pilot on the squadron, but his flying ability was well above average and he got on well with everybody. Young Reed would do all right.

Four of the squadron's pilots were NCOs, and they were top quality too. Yeoman looked at Flight Sergeant Miller, a wiry, hawk-faced man with dark eyes that had hidden depths to them. Like Sloane, Miller had completed a tour on Beau-fighters and had three German bombers to his credit, all at night. His navigator, Sergeant Sillitoe, who had come to Mosquitos with him, told horrifying stories of how Miller had yelled and cursed crazily in the cockpit as he pumped cannon shells into his shattered enemies at point-blank range, and now everyone knew the reason for his actions. For Miller was a Jew, sent to England from Germany by far-sighted parents in 1933 to be brought up by an aunt. The parents were to have followed, but they never did. Both were arrested and flung into a concentration camp, and Miller had no idea whether they were alive or dead. All he knew was that he had a highly personal score to settle with the Germans.

Once, in the sergeants' mess, he had remarked to Sillitoe that he would never allow himself to be captured alive if anything went wrong over enemy territory.

'Well,' his navigator had retorted mildly, 'that's up to you, old son. But if we catch it and you feel like diving the bloody thing into the middle of Berlin or somewhere, for Christ's sake let me get out first!' Together, they made a formidable team.

Then there was Flight Sergeant Lorrimer, the South African, who had spent his early working life as a merchant seaman (so many of his countrymen did, Yeoman mused). Lorrimer, sun-burnt and lithe, was a demon card player and a formidable drinker, although he seemed to sense when an operation was in the wind and never touched a drop for at least twenty-four hours beforehand. He had completed a tour in Coastal Command, flying Beaufort torpedo-bombers.

Sergeant Olafsson, the Icelander, was a typical Nordic type, blond and long-boned. He, too, was a former seaman, having served his apprenticeship on whalers, and had volunteered to serve with the British forces after Iceland was occupied by them in May 1940. Serving originally with the Air-Sea Rescue Service, Olafsson had applied for aircrew training and had been readily accepted. Like Lorrimer, he had completed a tour on Coastal Command Beauforts. Olafsson's nickname was 'Moby Dick', and Yeoman had a shrewd suspicion that it referred to something other than his association with whales.

Next to Olafsson sat the Icelander's close friend, Paddy Keen, a diminutive and wiry man of twenty-two who came from Rostrevor, in the north of Ireland. His shock of blond hair led Yeoman to believe that he might be descended from the Vikings who had settled in Northern Ireland nine hundred years ago; perhaps that accounted for the unlikely friendship between the two, for they seemed to have little else in common.

Last of all there was Sergeant Telfer, a man in his late twenties who had a wife and a couple of children somewhere up in County Durham. A quiet, pleasant individual, Telfer spent many hours alone in his billet, carving model aircraft out of perspex for his kids, but he was not reticent in the same way as O'Grady; his balding head gave him a fatherly appearance and Yeoman knew that the other NCOs often sought him out for advice, knowing him affectionately as

'Old Tcf'. A superb, rock-steady pilot, Telfer would never take unnecessary risks.

Yes, thought Yeoman, they were a good crew, just about the best a commander could wish for.

The engineer officer, the last of the specialists to speak, was concluding his part of the briefing with details of fuel loads and other technicalities, and when he had finished Yeoman rose to his feet and was joined on the platform by Group Captain Davison. The navigators had arrived outside and someone opened the door to admit them. When they were seated, Davison addressed the complete assembly.

'Well, gentlemen,' he began crisply, 'you have the details. It is now my job to put you in the overall picture. This morning, you will be operating in direct support of the United States Eighth Army Air Force.'

The crews exchanged glances, and a brief ripple of muted comment ran round the room. Davison picked up the billiard cue pointer and turned to the wall map.

'At 0600,' he went on, 'about a hundred and fifty Flying Fortresses will take off from their bases here in England to attack the Messerschmitt aircraft factory here, at Regensburg.' The tip of the pointer indicated a spot deep in Bavaria, five hundred miles inside enemy territory. There were low whistles from the audience. Five hundred miles into Germany. In daylight, with flak and fighters all the way. Not a recipe for survival.

The pointer's tip moved back across the map to the Frisian Islands, then inland again.

'The Fortresses will cross the Dutch coast here, and will have fighter escort to a point north of Meppel. After that, they will be on their own. As you can see, their route takes them across the centre of a line joining the three fighter airfields you have been detailed to attack.'

The group captain paused, then turned from the map to face the crews. 'This is where the enemy fighters are expected to start hitting them hard,' he said. 'If they can break through this heavily defended sector reasonably intact, then they will have a fighting chance of getting through to the target. After

55

attacking Regensburg, they will fly on to bases in North Africa.

'The Regensburg force will be followed by a second wave of over two hundred more Fortresses, whose target will be the ball-bearing factories here, at Schweinfurt.' The pointer tapped the map once again, then Davison went on: 'This second wave will not be required to penetrate so deeply into enemy territory. However, there is a snag. None of the Fortresses in the Schweinfurt force have been fitted with the necessary long-range fuel tanks to enable them to reach North Africa, which means that they will have to fight their way back over northern Germany and the Low Countries again.'

The group captain's hard gaze roved over the faces of the men in front of him. 'You must therefore see,' he continued, 'that any effort to disrupt the enemy's fighter defences may have a telling effect on the outcome of these two raids. If all goes well, your attack will take place some thirty minutes before the leading Fortresses cross the enemy coast, and we hope that you will be able to create enough confusion to keep a substantial proportion of the enemy fighters on the ground at the three designated airfields during the crucial period after the American fighter escort has turned back.

'By attacking half an hour ahead of the Fortresses, it is hoped that you will catch quite a number of enemy fighters being readied for take-off, out in the open and with their pants down. And remember this: every fighter you knock out could mean one more Fortress, and that means ten men will come back safely. That is all, gentlemen. Good luck to you all.'

Davison stepped down from the platform and the crews rose as he made his exit. As the door closed behind him, Yeoman said: 'Right, chaps. Now let's have a close look at those target photos.'

For the next twenty minutes, the crews pored over the photographs of their assigned targets, discussing the best methods of approach and attack. Yeoman decided to lead his four Mosquitos straight in from the north-west, at right-angles to Twenthe's main runway. They would attack in two pairs with a hundred yards between them horizontally, the second pair about four hundred yards astern of the first to give covering fire in case the leading aircraft were 'bounced'. The other two section leaders adopted a similar procedure.

They synchronized their watches; it was now 0450. All of them had already breakfasted, so there was nothing to do now but wait.

It was strange how, in the last minutes before taking off on operations, the grass always smelt sweeter, the air clearer. Small, insignificant things—the slow, unsteady flight of a bumble-bee, the call of a bird, even the trickle of a drop of moisture down a window-pane—all assumed a new importance, for always there was the knowledge, thrust deep into the recesses of the mind, that one might never see them again.

It was always so, even on a morning like this, when the air was chill and dank and the mist clung stubbornly to the ground, as though reluctant to yield to the rays of the rising sun. Yeoman, standing in the door of the dispersal hut, was worried about the mist; contrary to the Met people's predictions, it showed no signs of lifting. Visibility was barely sufficient for take-off, and no more—sufficient, that was, for a Mosquito. Yeoman, however, was not worried about his Mosquitos, but about the Flying Fortresses for which they were to breach a gap in the enemy's defences, for the Fortress needed a far longer take-off run than the Mosquito and he knew that the mist, which covered all Norfolk and Suffolk, was still too dense to allow the big American bombers to take off in safety. Laden as they would be with maximum fuel and high-explosive bombs, the Fortresses would need every available inch of runway.

For the fourth time, Yeoman rang the Met office to find out the latest situation, and received the same reply from the harassed duty officer: the mist would clear slowly as the sun came up. There might be a short delay in getting the main bomber force airborne, but nothing serious.

The pilot looked at his watch. He had already delayed 380 Squadron's take-off by ten minutes, to compensate at least in part for any hold-ups the Americans must be experiencing, but to delay any longer was to invite disaster, for by the time they arrived over enemy territory the Luftwaffe would already be wide awake.

He made up his mind and turned to the others. 'Well, lads,' he said simply, 'I suppose we might as well get on with it.'

Two by two, pilots and navigators, their parachutes draped over their shoulders, walked out across the damp grass to their aircraft, shadowy outlines in the gloom of the grey dawn. Yeoman stared out across the airfield and thought that he could just make out the shapes of the dispersal huts which had been erected for the use of the Mosquito night fighter squadron, whose arrival had apparently been delayed because of problems with the new AI equipment.

Yeoman's ground crew were standing by the Mosquito, and the corporal fitter came up to the pilot with the Form 700, the technical log that certified the aircraft fit to fly. Yeoman inspected it, then signed it.

'Everything's okay, then,' he said.

'Top line, sir,' the corporal replied cheerfully. 'There was a bit of a mag drop on the port engine, but that's fixed now. She'll go like a rocket.'

Satisfied, Yeoman walked round the aircraft, carrying out his external checks, then climbed the ladder and squeezed himself through the narrow hatch into the cockpit, followed by Hardy. Both men strapped themselves in and Yeoman went into the starting-up sequence, muttering the drill to himself, while Hardy sorted out his maps.

'Master switch, on. Voltmeter showing 24 volts. Bomb doors shut, selector neutral. Bomb control panel, all switches off, guard closed. Undercarriage: emergency knob in normal position, safety catch on. Air pressure okay, 200 p.s.i. Fuel cocks to outer tanks. Throttles one-half inch open, propeller speed controls fully forward, supercharger okay. Radiator flap switches closed, pressure venting on. Fuel transfer cock off, immersed fuel pump switch off.'

A glance through the perspex assured him that the ground crew were standing by the fuel priming pump, in case there was any trouble in starting up, but the engines had been run only half an hour earlier and priming ought not to be necessary.

He switched on the ignition, made a signal to the ground crew and then pressed the starter and booster-coil buttons for the port engine, watching the propeller. It began to turn, slowly at first, then its revolutions increased as the Merlin fired with a bang and a cloud of grey smoke. Yeoman repeated the process for the starboard engine; that, too, was soon roaring healthily. As soon as both engines were running, the pilot opened both throttles slowly to 1,200 rpm, checking temperatures, pressures and magnetos. As the oil and coolant temperatures rose satisfactorily, he checked the operation of the hydraulic pumps by opening up each engine to 2,000 rpm in turn and then lowering and raising the flaps. After testing the all-important magnetos again, this time at the take-off rpm, he throttled back and clipped his face mask into place, glancing over at Hardy. Over the intercom, he asked:

'Can you hear me okay, Happy?'

'Loud and clear, skip. We've just got a green from the caravan.'

Yeoman looked across towards the red-and-white control caravan. A green light, the signal to taxi, was flashing from it. The pilot glanced round to make sure that the other three Mosquitos in his section were ready; all their engines were turning and there was no abort signal. He made a list check of the controls and then waved the chocks away. One of the ground crew gave him the 'thumbs up' sign and he released the brakes, then opened the throttles a little. A last wave to the ground crew as the Mosquito began to move forward: they were on their way.

Ungainly on their big, robust undercarriages, lacking all grace until they entered their rightful element, the four Mosquitos of Yeoman's section waddled round the taxi track towards the end of Burningham's solitary runway, stopping just short of it while the pilots carried out their take-off checks. Yeoman decided to use fifteen degrees of flap and trimmed the elevators slightly nose-heavy to compensate for it; he also trimmed the rudder a little to the right to cancel out the Mosquito's slight tendency to swing in the opposite direction. The other checks were completed in seconds.

'All set, Happy?'

'Ready as I ever will be,' grunted the navigator. 'Course after take-off is zero-seven-zero degrees, magnetic.'

The light from the caravan was showing a steady green now, indicating permission to take off. Yeoman opened the throttles and turned on to the runway, aligning the Mosquito carefully with the centreline, then opened up to 3,000 rpm and let the aircraft have her head. Acceleration was fast, as always, and a light forward pressure on the control column was sufficient to bring the tail up. Then they were airborne, nosing up through the mist.

Yeoman raised the undercarriage and flaps and kept his hand firmly on the throttle levers until the needle on the airspeed indicator reached 200 mph. A patchwork of fields, roads and waterways, partially obscured by drifting patches of grey mist, swept by under the Mosquito's wings. Reaching forward, he turned the black knob under the altimeter until the QNH—the barometric pressure setting that indicated the aircraft's height above sea level—showed on the millibar scale. He would stay at just under two hundred feet for the time being, well clear of any obstacles on the flat East Anglian landscape, and then drop to a hundred feet over the sea.

The compass needle was steady on 070 degrees. The mist leaped at them in swathes, streaming over the cockpit canopy, above and below the wings. The slipstream from their propellers carved tunnels through it in their wake.

There was a hazy impression of rooftops, a confluence of roads, a cathedral spire, its base lost in the greyness.

'Norwich,' Hardy said. 'Coast coming up in four minutes.'

'Okay. Any sign of the others?'

Hardy craned his neck. 'Yeah. There's a Mossie about a hundred yards astern. It's Miller, I think. Can't see the others, though. Too murky.'

Yeoman was about to make a further comment when, suddenly, the cockpit was filled with blinding light. The intensity of it after the gloom made him gasp and he quickly lowered his smoked goggles, steadying the Mosquito on course with a rapid reflex action.

Ahead of them, steel-grey and limitless, stretched the sea, the horizon awash with sunlight. Behind them, stretching in a great arc along the curve of the coastline, the mist lay in low coils, and several thousand feet above it layers of broken cloud jutted out seawards. As Yeoman glanced back he saw the other three Mosquitos speeding in his wake and throttled back slightly, allowing them to catch up with him. Miller swung into position on his starboard quarter while Saint and Telfer took up station astern. As though held together by an invisible thread, the four Mosquitos dropped down to a hundred feet and streaked out over the waves towards the dangerous sky beyond the horizon.

Now that his eyes had grown accustomed to the light, Yeoman raised his goggles once more and glanced at his watch. It was now 0605 and they were making a ground speed of 220 mph, which meant that they would reach their turning-point off the Frisian Islands in thirty minutes, somewhat later than planned. Yeoman hoped the other two sections had got away all right.

Suddenly, the pilot leaned forward in his straps, peering intently at a smudge on the horizon. It was smoke, and as the Mosquito sped on he made out the distant outline of a ship, almost dead ahead. For a moment he toyed with the idea of changing course to avoid it, but then he reasoned that the vessel's lookouts would probably have sighted the formation already, so he decided to stick to the present heading.

There were in fact two ships, one some distance beyond the other and a mile or two astern. As they crept into sharper focus from the morning haze, Yeoman said:

'What do you make of 'em, Happy?'

Hardy shaded his eyes. The two ships had begun a sharp turn to starboard, pointing their bows towards the oncoming aircraft. 'Destroyers, I think,' the navigator said.

'Ours or theirs?'

'Hold on. I think they—yes, they're ours all right.'

Simultaneously, both men saw the White Ensign of the

Royal Navy fluttering over the stern of the nearer ship in the brief moments before the destroyer's grey, rakish lines swept past on their port side. A light winked from its bridge.

'They're wishing us good luck, skipper,' the navigator said. Yeoman waggled the Mosquito's wings in acknowledgement and then the ships were gone, dropping away astern, creaming away towards their unknown destination.

'At least their aircraft recognition's on the ball,' Yeoman said wryly. 'The last time I was anywhere near one of our ships, it nearly shot me out of the sky.'

The minutes ticked by, and they saw no more ships. From time to time, however, their shadows fleeted over the evidence of war; a patch of oil or floating wreckage, and once an upturned lifeboat. Nearly four years of conflict had turned the North Sea into a rubbish tip, the last resting place of millions of pounds' worth of scrap iron, the rusting carcasses of ships whose crumbling hulls cradled the bones of their crews. Aircraft, too, although they would be battered to pieces by the action of the tides far sooner, their fragments scattered and lost in the clinging mud.

Yeoman tore his mind away from morbid thoughts and checked his instruments, adjusting the throttle settings slightly. The other Mosquitos were still with him, their formation impeccable.

'Enemy coast ahead, skipper.'

There was a chill in those words that no amount of training or operational experience would remove. They produced a momentary iciness in Yeoman's spine, just as did that other term used in flying: the point of no return. They were lonely, fearful words, conjuring up realms of the unknown that might lie beyond them.

The long, straight coastline of Holland, hard to distinguish at first, rose slowly from the sea to the right of the Mosquito's nose. To the north of it, dark, hazy blobs, with a scattering of cloud hanging over them, resolved themselves into the islands of Texel and Vlieland.

'Nice work, skipper. Right on course.'

'Thanks, Happy. Keep your eyes skinned.'

The four Mosquitos drummed on, still at a hundred feet

and at times even lower. Safety lay in hugging the sea; the longer they escaped detection, the better their chances of survival. Away off their starboard wingtips, the long chain of Dutch islands crawled past with interminable slowness. Apart from what looked like a few fishing smacks, the sea was empty. So far, their luck was holding.

'We're abeam Terschelling now,' Hardy said, 'and that's Ameland coming up. Turning point in six minutes.'

'Roger. There's an aircraft at two o'clock, high. Can you make out what it is?'

Hardy stared out of his side of the cockpit. A long way above, over towards the coast, an aircraft crawled across the blue backdrop of the sky, heading in the opposite direction. It quickly receded into the distance.

'Twin-engined,' the navigator commented. 'Might have been a Junkers 88. Hard to tell at this distance. Anyway, he's gone. I don't think he could have spotted us.'

Yeoman rocked his wings in the pre-arranged signal that he was about to make a course alteration. Away to starboard, Flight Sergeant Miller rocked his own wings in acknowledgement and dropped back a little, giving the leader plenty of room.

'Stand by, skipper,' Hardy warned. 'Thirty seconds. New course one-six-nine magnetic. Fifteen seconds...five ...now!'

Yeoman brought the Mosquito round in a flat turn, still keeping as low as he dared, and levelled out on the new heading. The other three aircraft followed suit, jockeying into position again as they came out of the turn. Together, they roared over the drab, featureless strip of land that formed the narrow waist of Rottumerplaat Island and the pilots opened the throttles to full combat power as the mainland swept up to meet them.

Their shadows sped beside them as they leapfrogged over the dunes. Images flickered before Yeoman's eyes; a scattering of red-roofed cottages, a railway line, an isolated cyclist, waving frantically as he saw the roundels on their wings. Miraculously, there was no flak.

It was 0639, and they were plunging deeper into Holland

at a rate of four and a half miles every minute. Seventeen minutes to the target. There was no point in keeping radio silence now. Yeoman pressed the transmit button.

'Spanner Red aircraft from Spanner Leader. Spread out a bit. Watch out for flak to starboard.'

Only three miles to their right lay Groningen, and beyond it was Eelde, which McManners' section was scheduled to hit in a few minutes' time. They would pass very close to the railway junction to the south of Groningen, where there were known to be anti-aircraft defences. Yet still there was nothing; no vicious strings of fire racing up to meet them, no steel bursting across the sky in their path. It was as if the whole of Holland was asleep, but they knew it could not last.

They streaked over the placid, sun-dappled waters of a broad lake. There was a solitary boat in the middle of it, and as they flashed past Yeoman had a clear impression of its occupant raising what looked like a shot gun to his shoulder, and of the puff of smoke as he fired.

'Must be one of the enemy,' he said, voicing his thoughts aloud over the intercom with a chuckle.

'What?' asked Hardy, who had not seen the incident.

'Some bloke in a boat, blazing away at us with a shotgun.'

'Cheeky bastard,' the navigator grunted. 'I hope he fell in.'

Strangely, Yeoman felt completely relaxed. If it had not been for the terrain, they might easily have been on a low-level training flight over England. His right hand, gripping the control column, was firm but not tense; his left rested lightly on the throttle levers. The Mosquito was handling like a dream.

Beside him, Hardy was map-reading calmly, checking off the landmarks as they came up in front of the nose. At length, he announced:

'That's Emmen up ahead, skipper. Stand by to turn on to one-eight-five. Ten minutes to target.'

They had been flying a dog-leg course to give the impression that they were heading into Germany. Their new heading would actually take them past Nieuw Amsterdam and across the spit of German territory that jutted into northern Holland for ten miles or so; once clear of it they would be in sight of Twenthe, perfectly placed for a straight-in, low-level attack from the north.

For the last few minutes they had been flying over wooded terrain, dotted here and there with small villages. Now, as they made their brief incursion into Germany, the landscape changed subtly, becoming bare and marshy. Groups of workmen, cutting peat, scattered in all directions as the Mosquitos howled a few feet above their heads.

Hardy consulted his map. 'We're coming back into Holland,' he said. 'That's Ootmarsum, dead ahead. Ten miles to run.'

Quickly, Yeoman pulled the lever that opened the bomb doors and flicked the bomb selector switches on the instrument panel. The cannon and machine-guns were already armed. He pushed the throttles forward to combat rpm once more. A rapid glance around assured him that the other Mosquitos were properly positioned. He still couldn't see the target, but he knew it must be there, a couple of miles past the railway line that crossed his track from right to left.

He eased the stick back slightly to clear a copse of tall trees, and in that same instant Twenthe airfield burst into his vision: the stark outlines of the hangars on the far side, a cluster of buildings adjacent to them, a pattern of runways. For a split second of time the whole tableau seemed to hang there, frozen in the windscreen; then it dissolved in a blur of light and speed as the Mosquito bore down upon it.

Yeoman was barely conscious of the storm of fire that came at them from all sides, of the web of multicoloured lights, the strings of glowing shells from the quadruple 20-mm anti-aircraft guns, that interlaced over the surface of the airfield in their path. He was only vaguely aware of several terrific flashes close to the cockpit, of the rattle of splinters against the Mosquito's fuselage.

He held the aircraft straight and level, flying so low that the tips of the racing propellers almost clipped the grass, and headed straight towards one of the hangars. An aircraft, a

Focke-Wulf 190, suddenly appeared in front of him, its tail up as it sped down the runway. He fired, cannon and machine-guns together, and the 190 exploded in a gush of blazing fuel.

The Mosquito sped across the runway intersection, through the spreading ball of smoke and flame and débris, and Yeoman kept his thumb jammed down hard on the gun button. Ahead of the nose, the shells and bullets formed an avenue of exploding dust and earth.

A group of three Focke-Wulfs and a Junkers 88 stood outside the hangar. The shells danced over them; fragments whirled into the air and the Ju 88 collapsed on its belly.

The hangar loomed up hugely, its doors gaping wide. Beside Yeoman, Hardy pressed himself back into his seat, his face a frozen mask.

Yeoman pressed the bomb release, waited a fraction of a second until he heard the 'clunk' of the weapons falling away and then pulled hard on the stick. The Mosquito bounded skywards, clearing the hangar by feet.

The two 500-lb bombs, fitted with eleven-second delayed-action fuses, struck the hard standing just short of the hangar in a flat trajectory and bounced through the open door. One bounced again and tore its way through the far wall, continued its flight and embedded itself in the earthen wall that surrounded a communications building. The other ripped through several aircraft, lost its momentum and wedged itself between two supporting girders.

The Mosquito continued its rocketing climb, weaving clear of the flak. Yeoman suddenly realized that he was drenched in sweat.

'Are you okay, Happy?' he asked hoarsely. The navigator let out his breath in an explosive gasp.

'Jesus Christ, skipper!' he looked at his map and checked the figures he had pencilled on it earlier. 'Course for home on two-nine-zero.'

The new heading would take them straight out across Holland and the Zuider Zee, a distance of a hundred miles, keeping well to the north of the defences of Amsterdam and away from the hornet's nest that would now have been stirred up along their attacking route.

Yeoman pushed down the Mosquito's nose once more. Behind them, columns of smoke rose into the morning air over Twenthe. He pressed the R/T button.

'Red Section, acknowledge.'

Miller's voice came back immediately. 'Red Two, okay.'

Then, after a slight pause, came Terry Saint's New Zealand twang, distorted over the radio: 'Red Three, okay. Red Four's had it.'

'Poor old Tef,' Hardy said quietly.

'Are you certain, Red Three?' Yeoman asked.

'Yeah. Flew straight into a fuel bowser. Hell of a bang.'

Yeoman was silent for a second or two. Then he said: 'All right. Stick together, and stay low. Shoot up anything worthwhile you see on the way out, but don't waste ammunition. The fighters will be looking for us.'

The formation speared on at low level towards the broad band of the River Ijssel, their crews keeping a watchful eye on the sky. No fighters appeared, and Yeoman reasoned that they must be searching further to the north. He looked across at Miller's aircraft; its paintwork was scarred with jagged holes, and he supposed that his own must look much the same. It was a miracle that nothing vital seemed to have been hit.

They drummed over the outskirts of a town—Nijverdal—and flak opened up on them from two towers beside some sort of factory. Their speed quickly took them out of the danger area. A few minutes later they passed to the south of Zwolle, and soon afterwards they were crossing the flat polder that bordered the Zuider Zee, their strong dykes keeping the sea at bay. More flak rose to meet them as they crossed the Dutch coast, but it was inaccurate.

As they headed out to sea, Saint, who was bringing up the rear, reported two enemy fighters astern, but they were a long way away and although they followed the Mosquitos for some distance they were unable to close the gap. They eventually gave up the chase and turned back towards the coast, their specks dwindling in the far distance.

The Mosquitos landed at Burningham shortly after 0800 to find that the other two sections were already back. McManners was waiting for Yeoman as the latter climbed stiffly from his aircraft, and he carried bad news. Sloane was missing, down in the sea a few miles off the Dutch coast. Everyone else had returned safely with the exception of Lorrimer's navigator, who had collected a minor wound in his shoulder from a shell fragment. And, of course, poor Telfer.

There was more bad news to come, and it was broken by Group Captain Davison, who came out to greet the returning crews. Quietly taking Yeoman off to one side, he told him:

'I'm afraid there's been the most awful cock-up. The mist didn't clear fully until half an hour ago, and the Regensburg force is only just beginning to get airborne.' He glanced up at the cloud that still hung over East Anglia. 'I'm prepared to bet that they'll have problems getting their formations sorted out among that lot, too. What I'm saying is, the whole damned operation is about three hours behind schedule, and the Schweinfurt attack has been put off until this afternoon.'

Yeoman felt his heart sink. 'Why?' he asked.

'Because the Schweinfurt force, that's the 1st Bomber Wing, is operating from bases further inland, and the mist still hasn't cleared there yet. All the available escort fighters have been assigned to the Regensburg force, the idea being that they would keep the Luftwaffe busy while the Schweinfurt boys slipped through. Now that isn't possible, so they'll have to wait until the escorts get back from the first trip so that they can go along with the second as well.'

'What it all boils down to,' Yeoman said tiredly, 'is that the Jerries on the airfields we've just attacked will have had time to sweep up the pieces and get their fighters airborne to meet the Regensburg force.' He looked around at the battle-scarred Mosquitos, at the empty dispersals where Sloane's and Telfer's aircraft should have been standing, and a wave of utter dejection swept over him.

'What a bloody rotten waste!'

Chapter Five

'HERR MAJOR. HERR MAJOR! PLEASE WAKE UP, SIR!'

Richter groaned and turned over in bed, opening one bleary eye. The round, bespectacled face of his orderly, Corporal Singer, swam into focus.

'What's the matter?' Richter asked, his voice heavy with sleep. 'What time is it?'

'Six o'clock, sir.'

'In the morning?'

'In the morning.'

Richter struggled into a sitting position, rubbing a hand over his eyes.

'Damnation, Singer,' he snapped, 'I've only just got to bed. What the hell is going on?'

'I'm sorry, sir,' the corporal apologized. 'All I know is that all pilots are to report to operations as soon as possible. Even those who have been night flying. I've brought you some coffee, sir, and there's plenty of hot water.'

Richter nodded and swung his legs out of bed, reaching out for the mug of steaming black liquid. A few gulps cleared away some of the tiredness, and five minutes under a hot shower restored him to his normal self.

He dressed quickly, had a snack in the mess, thought briefly about calling a car to take him to the operations block, and then decided to walk. It was a fine morning, and he felt in need of some fresh air. The night's operations had been hectic and fruitless; the Tommies had sent over fast intruder aircraft in small numbers and Richter had been airborne twice, but neither he nor his pilots had made any contact.

Mosquitos, he thought, as he walked down the long avenue that led towards the airfield from the officers' mess, bordered with sweet-smelling pine trees. Always those infernal Mosquitos!

It was a week now since No. 2 Squadron, Fighter Wing 301, had moved from its primitive airstrip near Munster to Rheine-Hopsten, a well established airfield further to the north. Situated twenty miles from the Dutch border, Rheine possessed excellent facilities and a first-class organization under the command of Colonel Johann Sommer, a veteran of the Spanish Civil War. Sommer was a friendly man, always ready with a smile and a word of encouragement, but when it came to inefficiency he could be merciless.

Richter had taken an instant liking to him; the base commander reminded him of Werner Mölders, to whom Richter owed a great debt of gratitude; in the summer of 1940, at the start of the campaign in France, Richter—then a young and inexperienced pilot—had made a serious and humiliating mistake on his first operation, and it had been Mölders who had given him the strength to carry on. Richter felt a twinge of sadness when he remembered that Mölders was dead, killed in an air crash on his way back from the Russian Front; he had been the Luftwaffe's top-scoring fighter pilot at the time. It had seemed a senseless waste, for Mölders to die as a passenger in an aircraft flown by someone else; so much better if he had met his death cleanly, in air combat high above the earth.

He reached the operations block, exchanged salutes with the armed sentry at the entrance, and made straight for Sommer's office. He found the colonel seated at his desk in conference with three other officers, the commanders of the squadrons that shared Rheine with 2/JG 301.

'Good morning, Richter,' Sommer greeted him. 'My apologies for disturbing your sleep, but it looks as though we're going to need everyone we can lay our hands on today. Take a seat.'

Sommer placed his feet squarely on the desk top, leaned back and lit a long black cheroot. Through a cloud of smoke, he said:

'Our intelligence people have had a whisper that the Americans are planning something big—a simultaneous attack on different targets by two or even three waves of bombers, perhaps.' He got up suddenly and crossed over to a wall map, slapping it with a flourish. One of Sommer's very few failings was a slight tendency, at times, to be theatrical.

'Now, gentlemen,' he went on, 'we know that the enemy are giving considerable priority to attacks on our aircraft factories—in the past few weeks the Heinkel works at Rostock, the Fieseler plant at Kassel, the Focke-Wulf enterprises at Bremen and several others. One major aircraft production complex, however, has so far escaped unscathed, mainly because it lies deep in the Fatherland. I refer, gentlemen, to the Messerschmitt factories here, at Regensburg. Intelligence has indicated that the Americans have been planning an attack on this target for some time. I believe that it will take place today.'

He knows more than that, Richter thought. He has more information than we know about. Sommer was not the kind of man to make predictions lightly, without a sound basis of fact. The espionage network in Britain must have been working overtime lately; Richter guessed that certain information about the operational plans of the US 8th Bomber Command had leaked out and that the decision had been to pass it down the line to senior Luftwaffe commanders once it had been processed in Berlin.

Sommer saw the look in Richter's eye and smiled. 'Yes,' he admitted, 'we know they are coming, and that Regensburg is likely to be the target. Or at least one of the targets. We do not, as yet, know the identities of any others; nor do we know when the attacks will take place.'

The colonel took a long pull at his cheroot and spat out a shred of tobacco. 'However,' he continued, 'when they do

71

come we shall be waiting for them. The whole of Fighter Command on the Western Front is on the alert, and with any luck we'll hit the Amis so hard that they won't stick their noses into Germany for a long time.'

He was interrupted by the clamour of the telephone on his desk. He lifted the receiver, listened for a few moments and then spoke in brief acknowledgement before replacing the instrument.

'Well, gentlemen,' he said, 'that was Divisional Head-quarters. A few minutes ago, a small force of RAF Mosquitos carried out a low-level attack on the airfields of Twenthe, Hoogeveen and Eelde, in Holland. They inflicted consider-able damage. Divisional HQ is of the opinion that the attack was designed to create maximum confusion among our fighter defences in the north-west—to smash a hole through the wall, in other words. We might not have much time. I suggest that you bring your squadrons to immediate readiness.'

The four squadron commanders snapped to attention, sa-luted and left Sommer's office, heading for their various dispersals. Richter looked up at the sky, dappled here and there with high cloud. It was a beautiful morning, too beau-tiful for young men to die. But die many of them inevitably would, on both sides, before the sun reached its zenith.

The great formation of B-17 Flying Fortresses droned over the coast of Holland, glittering metallic insects sailing through clusters of flak. The time was ten o'clock, and the bombers were now almost four hours behind schedule. There were 147 of them, flying in seven tight boxes of twenty-one aircraft, stepped up between 17,000 and 19,000 feet. Any fighter seeking to penetrate any one of those boxes would have to run the gauntlet of up to 168 .5-in calibre machine-guns, for each Fortress was formidably armed with eight such weapons. There were no significant blind spots.

Above and ahead of the leading Fortress groups flew their fighter escorts, tubby P-47 Thunderbolts which would shep-herd them as far as the German border—but no further, for that was the limit of the Thunderbolt's radius of action even with auxiliary fuel. There should have been another group of P-47s, watching over the rearmost Fortress elements, but it had failed to make rendezvous because of a timing error. And it was the rearmost Fortress groups which were most vulnerable to attack.

To make matters worse, the rear groups began to trail badly as the formation flew deeper into Holland, until there were fifteen miles between them and the leading elements.

At 1017 the first enemy fighters were sighted. They were the Focke-Wulf 190s of No. 1 Fighter Wing and they shadowed the trailing Fortress groups at a respectable distance, making no move to attack. They had plenty of time. In just a few more minutes the Thunderbolt escorts would have to turn for home, and that would be the moment for the fighters to pounce.

The bomber crews sweated, and waited. Every few seconds, nervous gunners checked and re-checked their turrets and gun mechanisms, the long belts of ammunition that festooned the interior of the Fortresses like bronze snakes.

The leading Fortress groups changed course, heading southeastwards now as they approached the German border. Like a shoal of silvery fish, the Thunderbolts swung away from them on a heading that would take them back to their English bases, pushing down their noses to gather speed. Even if they were attacked, they would be hard pressed to defend themselves, for their margin of fuel was hardly sufficient for combat manœuvres.

But the Focke-Wulfs were not interested in the Thunderbolts. As the latter turned for home, the German fighter leader issued curt orders over the radio and the 190s broke away in pairs, plummeting down towards the rear Fortress groups. They attacked head-on, concentrating on the lowest squadron, and the American gunners had only a fraction of a second in which to bring their sights to bear as the Focke-Wulfs flashed through the formation at 400 mph.

The bombers shuddered to the recoil of their machine-guns. Spent cartridge cases sprayed across the floors and the air inside the vibrating fuselages was thick with cordite fumes.

Intercoms were choked with excited, high-pitched voices as the gunners called out the positions of the fighters, now coming in from all round the clock.

A Fortress dropped slowly out of formation, its fuselage shattered by cannon shells, its controls shot away. It went over on its back and fell earthwards in a ponderous spin, shedding fragments of wing. Two parachutes broke clear, to vanish almost instantly in a great burst of smoke and flame as the bomber exploded.

Two more Fortresses dropped away within seconds of each other, both streaming flames from their wings. Long columns of black smoke marked their final plunge.

The fighters made three savage, high-speed attacks and then were suddenly gone, dwindling against the drab earth as they headed back to their bases to refuel and re-arm. Two of them had been shot down by the Fortress gunners; it was impossible to fly through that storm of fire and emerge completely unscathed.

Away to the right of the American formation, higher up and well clear of the guns, flew a lone Junkers 88. This was the Fighter Director, whose task was to report any sudden changes of course and also observe any weak spots which the Focke-Wulfs and Messerschmitts might exploit. Already, dozens more were climbing hard to join the battle.

The time was 1032, and the Fortresses were now entering Germany.

Joachim Richter was sprawled in a deckchair, dozing fitfully in the warm sunshine within easy sprinting distance of his Messerschmitt, when the alarm klaxon sounded. Instantly wide awake, it took him only seconds to cover the intervening yards of ground and swing himself into the cockpit, before the Gustav's big three-bladed propeller spun into life.

Rheine airfield was a confusion of taxi-ing aircraft. There must have been at least forty of them, Focke-Wulf 190s, Messerschmitt 109s and a few twin-engined Messerschmitt 110s—the latter with 21-cm rockets mounted in underwing tubes—all jockeying for position. There was no time for the niceties of an orderly take-off, flight by flight, squadron by squadron; the thing was to get off the ground as quickly as possible and climb like hell in order to get above the incoming Fortresses, the fighters sorting themselves out into combat formations on the way up.

The latest report was that the Americans had made a series of course alterations, taking them well to the south of their expected route. They were now in the vicinity of München-Gladbach. Richter made a quick mental calculation and ordered his squadron on to a heading that should permit them to intercept the bombers some distance to the south of Cologne.

They caught up with the rear groups of Fortresses at 1055. Still climbing, Richter brought his squadron round in a wide curve, passing right over the top of the American formation to place his Messerschmitts ahead of it and several thousand feet higher up.

Dropping one wing briefly, he looked down and, from his vantage point, gained a clear impression of the havoc already wrought on the Fortresses by the non-stop fighter attacks. It was easy to pick out the great gaps in the Americans' ranks, particularly among the lower squadrons, and he could see smoke trailing from the engines of at least two other B-17s.

Even as he watched, he saw a Messerschmitt 110 make a beam attack on three Fortresses, its pilot flying straight and level through meshes of tracer. Plumes of smoke burst from behind the 110's wings and for an instant he thought it had been hit, but then he realized that it had launched its salvo of rockets. The missiles' white smoke trails, clearly visible, bridged the gap between the fighter and one of the Fortresses with incredible speed and disappeared into the bomber's bowels.

There was a blinding flash, followed by a rolling ball of flame as the B-17's bomb load exploded. The accompanying smoke cloud reached out to engulf the neighbouring Fortresses, which sheered wildly away from it. Richter saw the Fortress's four engines fall from the cloud and drop like stones, each trailing its own ribbon of smoke. The tail section fluttered down, turning over and over, its silver surfaces reflecting the sun.

By this time the Messerschmitts were well ahead of the enemy formation.

'Attention,' he called over the radio, 'Elbe Leader to Elbe Squadron, execute frontal diving attack in pairs. Concentrate on low groups. Go!'

Followed by his wingman, Sergeant Thiel, he rolled the Messerschmitt on its back and pulled on the stick, streaking down in a vertical dive and easing out of it on a level with the lowest squadron of Fortresses. The fighters sped like arrows at the leading flight of bombers. Richter picked a target and centred the luminous dot of his sight on the bomber's nose. Spidery grey lines leaped at him from the Fortress's front guns, flickered over his wings and cockpit. He resisted a desperate urge to shut his eyes and squeezed the triggers of his cannon, keeping them depressed until the very last moment. Then he pushed forward the stick and kicked the rudder bar, sending the Messerschmitt skidding under the bomber's port wing, ducking involuntarily as its dark oil-streaked shadow passed a few feet above his head.

Richter held the fighter in the dive for a few seconds, building up speed, then pulled up into a steep climb, looking back. The Fortress he had just attacked was still in formation. He swore and sought another target, noting as he did so that Thiel had come through unscathed and was climbing up to join him. Both fighters levelled out, cruising a few thousand feet above and behind the formation. The other Messerschmitts were ripping through it, but as yet no Fortresses were going down.

'There's a straggler, Thiel, below and to the left,' Richter radioed. 'Let's finish him off. Attack from astern.'

The Fortress Richter had singled out was dragging a thin streamer of smoke, barely discernible, from its starboard outer engine. He closed right in astern of it, ignoring the fire that poured at him from the bomber's turrets, and systematically began to chop it to pieces with short bursts from his cannon. He saw his shells punch holes in the Fortress's rear fuselage, and an instant later the ventral ball turret disintegrated in a tangle of perspex, metal and shattered human flesh as his shells found their mark there too.

The Messerschmitt shuddered and holes suddenly appeared in its port wing; the American rear gunner was a good shot, and Richter knew that he had to dispose of him. Taking infinite care, he lined up his sights on the man's turret. His finger curled around the trigger.

A series of terrific bangs shook the Messerschmitt in rapid succession. The side panel of the cockpit canopy vanished in a spray of razor-sharp particles and the left side of the pilot's face suddenly became numb. Simultaneously, something struck his left leg a violent blow, jerking his foot off the rudder pedal.

The port wing dropped sharply, and before Richter could correct it the Gustav fell into a tight spiral dive. He forced his foot back on to the rudder pedal and took recovery action; the Messerschmitt responded sluggishly and he managed to bring it back into level flight, although he had to keep the stick well over to the right to stop the port wing dropping again.

'Elbe Leader, are you all right?' Thiel's voice crackled over the radio, urgently and full of concern.

'Elbe Two, Victor... I think so.'

Cautiously, he explored the side of his face with his fingertips. They came away reddened with blood, but he felt no pain. There was just an overwhelming feeling of relief: thank God his eyes were undamaged. Looking down, he found a tear in the thigh of his flying overall and poked a finger through that, too, withdrawing it quickly when a shaft of pain stabbed through his whole leg. It was replaced by a strong tingling sensation, and relief came once again when he discovered that he could feel his foot. The damage did not appear to be too great, but there could be no question of rejoining the combat, for he was having trouble in controlling the aircraft. He had to find somewhere to land, and quickly.

'Elbe Leader to Elbe Squadron, am breaking off.'

The voice that acknowledged him was that of Johnny Schumacher. High above, the other Messerschmitts were still tearing into the Fortresses, making the most of it while their fuel and ammunition lasted. Two of the big bombers had already gone down in flames before their guns, and Sergeant Thiel, having killed the troublesome rear gunner, was disposing of a third.

Richter glanced at his altimeter; he was at four thousand metres, nosing down through patches of cloud. He was flying over hilly, densely wooded country, laced with streams and tiny lakes. Far off to the left was the Rhine, with the smoky patch of Cologne on the northern horizon. Following the course of the river southwards with his eyes, he located Bonn and its neighbouring town of Bad Godesberg and decided to make for Bonn-Hangelar airfield. If he could not get that far, there was a chance that he might be able to put the crippled Messerschmitt down at Eudenbach, a small airstrip which lay on his route.

The Westerwald, all variegated shades of greens and browns, crawled slowly beneath his wings. From time to time an alarming shudder shook the aircraft and his hand tensed on the stick, ready to take instant corrective action, but each time the tremor ceased after a second or two. The port aileron appeared to be buckled, responding only marginally to his control movements.

The side of his face was stinging abominably, as though it was suffering from a hundred small razor cuts. He put up an exploratory hand and found that the bleeding had stopped, thanks probably to the stream of air that flowed into the cockpit through the shattered side panel. His left thigh was also throbbing badly; it felt as though he had been kicked by a mule.

A wave of nausea swept over him and he turned his oxygen fully on, feeling his head start to clear as the cool gas played against his face. The needle of the altimeter unwound steadily. Below, a broad, straight autobahn sliced through the forest, running parallel with the Rhine and leading like an artery to the Ruhr Valley; he kept it in sight off his port wingtip, knowing that Eudenbach lay a few kilometres to the west of it. The Messerschmitt was becoming more difficult to control with every passing minute, and he now knew for certain that he was not going to reach Bonn.

Landing was going to be tricky. He had already tried the emergency frequency, but the radio had gone dead soon after he began his descent. With no chance of making a proper nonradio approach, he would just have to go straight in and hope for the best.

Eudenbach appeared ahead, a grassy patch surrounded by woods. Richter throttled back, changed the propeller pitch and pulled the undercarriage lever.

Nothing happened. There was no reassuring thud as the main wheels came down and locked into place. Two red lights on the instrument panel flickered on and stayed on, glowing at him mockingly. He pumped the lever several times, again with no result.

He began to sweat. Whether the undercarriage was still locked in the 'up' position, or whether it was partly down, he had no means of knowing. In the latter case, the Messerschmitt would certainly flick over on its back if he tried a belly landing. But he had no choice; he was now too low to bale out, and the degree of control was so marginal that an attempt to climb might prove fatal.

He took a deep breath and pulled at his straps, making them as tight as possible. Cautiously, he lowered a few degrees of flap and pointed the fighter's nose at a point about one-third of the way along the grass strip.

Trees swept past on either side. As he crossed the airfield boundary, he quickly switched off the engine and feathered the propeller. There was a blurred glimpse of some buildings, with a few small aircraft parked beside them. The grass flowed under his wings and he began to ease back the control column, as gently as he could. The Gustav floated for what seemed an endless distance and then hit the ground with a crunch that jarred every bone in his body. The straps bit into his shoulders cruelly as the sudden deceleration threw him forward in the cockpit; he let go of the stick and raised both arms to protect his face. Something struck him a violent blow on the head, partly stunning him. The noise of rending metal was fearful.

He sat there, his shoulders hunched, his arms still crossed over his face, for long seconds before he realized that the noise had ceased. Opening his eyes, he looked around him dazedly. In front of him, the engine cowling was a crumpled mass of metal, with wisps of smoke coming from it. The port wing had broken off half-way along its length. There was an overpowering smell of petrol.

Stirring himself with difficulty, he yanked at the latch that secured the cockpit hood and pushed upwards at the metal frame. The square-cut canopy came free with a grating sound and dropped over to one side. Fresh air, mingled with the smell of aluminum and scorched rubber, washed over him. He struggled to unfasten his seat harness and parachute. Hands were reaching down into the cockpit, seizing him by the arms, dragging him clear. He tried to speak, but his mouth was so dry that he could only manage a faint croak. Two men each got one of his arms over their shoulders and helped him across the grass to an ambulance. A third rolled up the sleeve of his flying overall and tried to insert a needle into his arm; Richter shoved the man's hand away, trying to tell him that he was all right, that his blood-caked face looked worse than it really was.

With a supreme effort, Richter pushed aside the restraining hands and managed to stand upright on trembling legs, fighting the throbbing in his thigh. Then the grass came up and hit him in the face and he knew no more.

'Is the Major feeling better now?'

Richter opened his eyes fully and focused on the smiling face of the man who bent over him. He was a lieutenant, and his insignia showed that he was a member of the Luftwaffe's medical branch.

He held out something in the palm of his hand and showed it to the pilot. It was a bullet, slightly flattened at the nose.

'We dug that out of your thigh,' he said. 'You were very lucky. It must have spent itself as it entered your aircraft's cockpit; it was lodged just under the skin. The cuts on your face were only superficial, too. We've cleaned them up. However, you got a nasty bang on the head when you crash-landed, that's why you passed out. You might have a headache for a day or two, but there's no permanent damage.'

'Is there anything to drink?'

The lieutenant offered him a small glass and he drank the contents down in a single gulp, coughing slightly; it was neat brandy.

'That will bring the blood back to your cheeks,' the lieutenant said. 'There's also some coffee in the pot over there, on the table. You can get up, if you want to. Take it easy, though; you'll probably feel a little groggy.'

Richter threw aside the blanket that covered him and swung his legs over the side of the bunk, wincing as he did so. His head hurt abominably and his thigh was stiff; there was a bandage round it.

'You'll have quite a bruise there, sir,' the lieutenant said cheerfully. 'Your uniform is over there, in the locker. We've already been in touch with your unit, and we'll arrange an aircraft to fly you back later this afternoon. In the meantime, perhaps you would like something to eat? I can easily arrange for some food to be sent over from the mess.'

Richter dressed and went outside. An orderly brought a chair and he relaxed gratefully in the warm afternoon sun, eating a little cold meat and salad. Eudenbach, he soon discovered, was used by a communications flight consisting of six aircraft, a mixed collection of Fieseler Storches and twin-engined Focke-Wulf Weihes; their comings and goings did little to disturb the peace. After a while, he dozed off.

The two hundred and thirty Flying Fortresses bound for Schweinfurt came thundering in over the mouth of the Scheldt, and this time the squadrons of Messerschmitts and Focke-Wulfs did not wait for the Thunderbolt escort to turn back, but came boring in from high altitude to take on both bombers and fighters. They dived out of the sun, streaking through the top groups of Fortresses and continuing down through the American formations to strike the lower groups at a speed that took them clear of the gunners in seconds. The first B-17s tumbled from the sky to scatter their smoking wreckage over the Dutch countryside; the rest closed up the gaps in their ranks and droned on, their crews conscious that their ordeal was only just beginning. Many of them would reach the target; but after that would come the long flight back across north-west Europe, fighting for survival every inch of the way.

The massed roar of their engines shook Richter from his doze and brought him stiffly from his chair, peering into the bright southern sky. Far to the south, glittering in the sun, he clearly saw the crawling procession of metallic dots and followed them for several minutes before they were lost to sight. Not all of them, for a twisting streamer of black smoke, barely thicker than a thread of cotton at this distance, marked a bomber's last plunge.

A squadron of Focke-Wulfs howled overhead, climbing hard, heading at full throttle for the battle that was raging four miles over Germany. for the victorious squadrons of the Luftwaffe, the day was far from over.

Nor was it over for the Mosquitos of No. 380 Squadron. Early in the evening of that bitter, tragic 17 August, they were ordered into the air to patrol the route of the homecoming bombers over Belgium, quartering the sky in pairs at up to 25,000 feet. The sky was full of fighters; squadrons of American Thunderbolts and Lightnings and RAF Spitfires, all hurrying to the assistance of the hard-pressed bombers.

Yeoman, whose Mosquito was flanked by Miller's, saw them first as he flew high to the south of Brussels. The bombers were leaving broad vapour trails, and as he headed towards them Yeoman saw that their formations were split by the more slender streaks left by the speeding enemy fighters. Twisting air battles were going on all around the battered Fortress groups as the Thunderbolts, well out in advance, went full tilt at the Luftwaffe as though seeking to make up for their absence during those terrible, hard-fought hours over Germany. From all directions, the allied fighter squadrons were converging on those few tortured square miles of sky; Yeoman counted at least seventy Spitfires at various points around the clock, and on one occasion a squadron of Lockheed Lightnings, easily identifiable by their twin tail booms, their noses painted with crimson sharks' teeth, sniffed inquisitively at the Mosquitos before making off. It was a timely reminder that, from certain angles, the Mosquito could look uncannily like a Junkers 88; they would have to watch their step, especially when they got near the bombers, for the gunners were likely to be exceptionally trigger-happy.

The Thunderbolts and Spitfires, sweeping round behind the straggling squadrons of Fortresses, appeared to be doing a good job of driving off the remaining enemy fighters, so Yeoman ordered his Mosquitos to take up station on the flanks of the American formation, cautioning the pilots to keep well out of range of the B-17s' guns.

They could see, now, that almost all the Fortresses had sustained battle damage. Yeoman edged in carefully towards one bomber which seemed to be losing height steadily; it was in a pitiful state, its wings and fuselage blackened by smoke, punctured by shells and bullets, and as Yeoman watched he saw that the crew were throwing loose objects through the escape hatches in a desperate attempt to lighten the aircraft. But one engine had already gone and smoke was trickling from another, and Yeoman knew deep inside him that it was no use, that the Fortress would not make it back across the Channel.

Certain now that the Mosquito had been identified, he closed right in until he was flying wingtip to wingtip with the crippled bomber, as though the presence of a friendly fighter so close to hand might give the American crew hope and encouragement, the extra reserves of strength that would enable them to keep the Fortress flying by sheer willpower. The Belgian coast was almost under their noses now, and although the Fortress was now losing height so quickly that a ditching in the English Channel was inevitable, its pilot might at least be able to set it down close to home.

Flak bayed at them as they crossed the coast near De Panne, but only the last burst came anywhere near them and they were soon clear, heading due west. Away to the left lay Dunkirk, the scene of battles of earlier days, and dead ahead of them, hazy under the falling sun and tantalizingly close, was the coast of Kent.

'He's had it, skipper,' Hardy said quietly. The navigator was right; the Fortress was going down quickly now, with only one engine turning, and that too stopped as the American pilot levelled out a few feet above the waves. An instant later the big bomber was down, slewing across the water in gouts of foam.

Yeoman brought the Mosquito round in a climbing turn and put out a distress call, looking down as he did so. The B-17's nose section was awash, and although the bomber was floating it would not remain buoyant for long, as water was pouring into it through the open escape hatches.

'They seem to be getting out all right,' the pilot commented. He could see tiny figures on top of the B-17's fuselage. 'There are the dinghies. Yes, they seem to be okay; they're getting into the dinghies now.'

Slowly, the sea closed over the top of the Fortress until only part of the rear fuselage, surmounted by the big tailfin, was left above the surface. Then that too was gone, leaving a swirl of eddying water on which the two orange dinghies bobbed.

Yeoman swept low over them while Hardy counted the heads of the occupants. There were only six of them, and a B-17 carried a crew of ten. Four men, probably dead already, had gone to their last resting place on the sea bed in the metal coffin of their aircraft.

The Mosquito continued to circle the dinghies until a pair of Thunderbolts arrived to take over; an air-sea rescue launch would be on its way before long. The valiant air-sea rescue boys, Yeoman thought as he set course for home, must have been badly overworked today, with Fortresses ditching all over the place.

The full extent of the tragedy of 17 August would not be known for some time, until the losses of the Regensburg force, its surviving bombers now safe on their North African airfields, filtered through to VIII Bomber Command Headquarters. The total cost to the Americans was sixty Flying Fortresses, with a further hundred damaged by flak or fighters. Some of the bomber groups, particularly those involved in the Schweinfurt attack, had lost ten or eleven aircraft out of twenty-one.

It had, as Hardy remarked as he and Yeoman walked away from their Mosquito at Burningham, been a hell of a day, and a costly one for 380 Squadron too, with one crew dead and another missing. He told Hardy to ask the mess stewards to put some food aside for him and went straight to his office; there were reports and letters to be written, the letters most painful of all, for it was impossible to dispose of human lives and to comfort grieving relatives with a few short words.

He sat down behind his desk and pulled a sheet of paper towards him. He let his chin rest on his hands and stared down at the blank page for a long time. Suddenly, he felt unutterably lonely.

Chapter Six

FLIGHT LIEUTENANT FREDDIE BARNES ADJUSTED HIS GLASSES
and settled down to re-read the last few pages of the Squadron
Diary, the day-to-day life of RAF Burningham chronicled in
his own neat copperplate handwriting. The entry for 18 August, the day after the Regensburg and Schweinfurt disasters,
gave him immense satisfaction. The entry began, in capital
letters:

'GOOD NEWS! Flight Lieutenant Sloane and his navigator,
Pilot Officer Wedgewood, are safe, having been brought
in by Air-Sea Rescue after an uncomfortable day and night
in their dinghy. It seems that as Sloane was crossing the
Dutch coast on his way home something, presumably flak,
hit his aircraft in the port engine. No gun flashes were
seen, and it would appear that this was one lucky burst.
A small fire broke out and was soon extinguished, but then
the oil pressure in the starboard engine began to rise and
there was a considerable loss of airspeed.

'After about five minutes on 272 degrees magnetic at
sea level, however, the starboard engine became considerably steadier and the Mosquito, which had so far persistently refused to climb above four hundred feet, now
began to gain altitude at a steady 150 knots Indicated Air

86

Speed until it reached 5,000 feet some thirty miles off the Dutch coast. Sloane then contacted Burningham Control, saying that he was in distress and would probably have to ditch. Soon afterwards, oil began to pour from the starboard engine, accompanied by rough running.

'Sloane decided to try and get as close to the English coast as possible, but after five more minutes the starboard engine packed in altogether. He followed the recommended ditching drill, jettisoning the roof panel and lowering flaps 25 degrees. The Mosquito touched down at about 80 knots, the rear fuselage underside striking the water first. The landing was trouble-free and the aircraft subsequently remained afloat for approximately fifteen seconds. The navigator made his exit first and Sloane made to follow, but he had some difficulty in unfastening his harness and the cockpit was underwater by the time he succeeded. Holding his breath, he pushed himself clear of the roof hatch with both hands and, since he was not a strong swimmer, immediately inflated his Mae West. Pilot Officer Wedgewood had already inflated the L-type dinghy and both men climbed into it after expending a fair amount of energy, for a considerable swell was running.'

The two men had seen several aircraft in the course of the day, but although they had tried to attract their attention, none had come near. It was not until the following morning that they had been picked up by a Westland Walrus amphibian of the Air-Sea Rescue Service, whose crew, out searching for survivors of a downed Lancaster, had come upon them purely by chance.

During the night, Sloane and Wedgewood, both wet and miserably seasick, had heard what sounded like hundreds of heavy bombers passing overhead in the darkness, returning a few hours later. The following morning, they learned that six hundred aircraft of Bomber Command had raided Peenemünde, on the Baltic coast of Germany, where the enemy had some sort of secret establishment. The attack had apparently been a complete success, although forty bombers had failed to return.

In view of the events of 17 August, Barnes wondered if No. 380 Squadron's Mosquitos might have been more usefully employed as night intruders in support of the RAF raid, rather than the American daylight attacks. They could certainly have remained in the vicinity of the German fighter bases for much longer under cover of darkness; operating singly, they could have covered a dozen airfields in northern Germany, sowing confusion at a time when the bombers were approaching the target area. Still, he thought resignedly, it was not his place to question the wisdom of the planners at Group HQ and higher.

Barnes took a sip from the mug of tea at his elbow and read on, picking extracts at random. Generally speaking, the squadron's operations during the last two weeks of August had been pretty routine.

'21.8.43. Total of eight sorties: shipping recce and cannon tests. The reconnaissance was carried out by Saint, O'Grady, Reed and Olafsson, who sighted a large convoy off Texel consisting of about twenty ships steaming in two lines ahead, some ships carrying balloons. A strike was immediately laid on by Coastal Command, but we have no information on the outcome.

'23.8.43. Total of twenty-two sorties. In the morning there was drogue towing, air-to-air and air-to-sea firing, camera gun practice and camera tests, and in the afternoon there was a sweep over Ijmuiden. There was a most unfortunate accident in the morning when a visiting Martinet, which was here for drogue towing, apparently took off in coarse pitch and crashed into a tree. The pilot was injured, though not seriously, but his passenger was killed. A Court of Inquiry is pending.

'In the afternoon the squadron made rendezvous with twelve Lockheed Venturas over North Walsham and the formation flew at sea level to within a few miles of the Dutch coast, climbing to 9,000 feet over Ijmuiden. As we crossed the coast four FW 190s were seen breaking cloud below at 2,000 feet. Our allotted task was to give top

88

cover to the bombers which, instead of bombing imme-diately, went inland for ten minutes then turned round and bombed from east to west on an outward heading. Squad-ron Leader Yeoman decided not to go down for the 190s until the bombers had carried out their task, or while they were still in danger of being attacked. While the bombers and escorts were making their incursion the 190s climbed up and were joined by others, but before they could attack the bombers they were engaged by 380 Squadron. In the resulting dogfight, of which no-one seemed to have a very clear picture, Sergeant Keen destroyed an FW 190 which he followed down to sea level and set on fire; it was eventually seen to crash into the sea by Flight Sergeant Miller.

'Miller himself was attacked and his aircraft hit, and he in turn claimed a FW 190 damaged. Squadron Leader Yeoman, who engaged the leading FW 190, also claimed one damaged, the enemy aircraft breaking away after being hit by cannon fire and going down followed by Pilot Of-ficer Saint, who lost sight of it. Saint was attacked head-on by two FW 190s, but was not hit. All our aircraft re-turned with the exception of one Ventura, which was hit by flak over the target.

'25.8.43. Bad weather, so no flying apart from a few circuits carried out by Flying Officer O'Grady, carrying out a weather check. Flight Lieutenant McManners went off on a long overdue week's leave, catching the milk lorry in Downham Market at 0700. This certainly is a foul place to get away from when going on leave, and even harder to get back to. We feel that if the general public realized how badly the Services are treated in matters of this sort, they would be more than surprised; it is a very serious problem that needs to be looked into by the au-thorities. Most of us live a long way from here. We are not allowed Service transport to take us to a convenient railway station, and the only convenient station in the whole of East Anglia is Norwich. Everywhere else, the train services are hopeless. It is particularly hard for family men, who have such matters as children's schooling to see to. A 48-hour leave is spent almost entirely on the train by most of us.'

Barnes scanned the lines again, surprised by his own vehemence. Yet it was true; servicemen going on leave had a rotten deal, at any rate in the British forces. The Americans were far better organized, with transport laid on. After all, the whole idea of going on leave was to return to operations refreshed, not exhausted as the result of long, sweaty hours packed like sardines on a dirty train.

Neither were the frustrations confined on going to leave. In other areas, too, niggling organizational problems tended to assume an importance out of all proportion. The diary continued:

'There was a dance at a place called Camp O in the evening. Having been promised a bus after much wrangling, which we were to share with some Air-Sea Rescue blokes, and after having dined early and been all set for the party, some idiot in ops rang us at the mess and told us that we had to call at an Army camp up the road and get a whole band on too. This was too much for Terry Saint and Yves Romilly, who decided not to go at the last moment. Terry became most awkward, and hid himself in the billiard room. Using his well-known tact, the writer managed to coax him out again, only to find that the bus had gone without us. We therefore had a game of billiards, drank several beers, and then decided to go boldly forth into the night to look for Camp O in my car. We motored all over the countryside, but never found the wretched place. We heard afterwards that it was a rotten dance, so we didn't miss much.'

The next entry recorded that on 26 August, a fresh crew had arrived to replace Telfer and his navigator. The new pilot was a big, broad-shouldered Canadian Warrant Officer named Arthur Laurie who, to nobody's surprise, turned out to have been a lumberjack before joining the RCAF. His navigator,

Sergeant John Trevarrow, was a soft-spoken Cornishman. As a team they had already flown a tour on Mosquito light bombers and were highly experienced.

'28.8.43. Total of nineteen sorties: camera gun and low flying practice, and an extremely shaky sweep to Utrecht in foul weather. Rendezvous with fifteen Venturas was made over Yarmouth and course set for Utrecht, but on reaching the Dutch coast the weather had deteriorated to such an extent that the bomber leader decided to return, the target being obscured. We were flying top cover and a squadron of Spitfires close escort. Something went wrong with the bomber leader's navigation on the way back, and he followed a course of 310 degrees magnetic, which would have brought the formation back over the English coast much too far north, somewhere near Hull. When we were forty miles from the English coast Squadron Leader Yeoman dived in front of the Venturas, waggling his wings since there was no radio contact, but the bombers and the Spits held their course so the co brought 380 Squadron on to a westerly heading and eventually crossed the coast near Cromer, returning to base at low level under the cloud base. The Venturas and their Spitfire escort apparently landed all over the place.

'30.8.43. An unusually cold morning, with a scramble by two Mosquitos at 0800. The pilots involved were Keen and Lorrimer, who went off to chase a suspected Hun raider off the Norfolk coast. The Hun turned out to be a Heinkel 111, engaged in mine-laying operations; our chaps made short work of it and claimed half a kill each.

'Squadron Leader Yeoman has been in unusually high spirits for several days now. We think he has had some good news, but despite all our efforts he will not say what it is. He goes off on seventy-two hours' leave tomorrow, so maybe that has something to do with it.'

Yeoman turned off the main road and relaxed behind the wheel of his little Morgan sports car, sweeping her effortlessly round corners and revelling in the evening sunshine. The road was just as he remembered it, flanked by harvest fields, with the land rising gently to the west to meet the foothills of the Pennines. He pressed his foot on the accelerator and whistled softly through his teeth. The air, battering around the sides of the windscreen, was soft and cleansing on his face. Nineteen hundred years earlier, Roman legions had tramped along this stretch of road on their way to the chain of fortlets that linked York with the west coast.

His companion snuggled close to him and kissed him lightly on the cheek.

'You sound happy,' she murmured.

'I am happy,' he smiled. 'I still can't believe that you're here with me. After all this time. I'd given you up, especially when there was no word from you.'

'I'm glad you didn't, though. And I did write, as I told you. I don't know what can have happened to the letters.'

He gave her a swift sidelong glance. She was smiling quietly to herself, her red hair flowing out in the slipstream. She wore a light green uniform, with the silver bars of a lieutenant, us Army, on the lapels and shoulder flashes that proclaimed her trade of war correspondent.

'It doesn't matter,' he said. 'About the letters, I mean. All that matters is that you're safe, and that we're together again, if only for the time being.'

'Don't say that.' She turned her green eyes towards him, and he melted. 'Don't say that, George. We're not going to lose each other again. I'm in England now, for the duration. We'll be able to see each other as often as we can.'

He made no reply. So much time had elapsed since he had last seen her; there had been so much heartache in the beginning, followed by a long grey time when he had cared about nothing other than survival; then there had been Malta, and solace for a few short moments with someone else, oases of peace amid the frightful strain of constant air combat. What he felt now, towards Julia Connors, was difficult to analyse. He needed time to sort out his scrambled emotions; they both did.

All they knew, for the moment, was that they were happy.

He, for his part, had no wish to make promises he might not be able to keep.

They came to a village, with grey-walled cottages nestling around the perimeter of the traditional village green. On the far side, its whitewashed walls standing out conspicuously in the evening sunlight, was an inn. Yeoman glanced quickly at his watch; their destination was only half an hour away, the evening was still young, and nothing would be lost if they stopped for a while.

'Let's have a beer or two,' he said, pulling the Morgan off the road and switching off the ignition. He climbed out, stretching his legs gratefully, and went round the car to open the other door for Julia. They paused for a moment together, looking into the rippling waters of a small stream that wound its way past the green and disappeared behind the inn. Clouds of midges danced over the surface and swallows darted through them, flicking this way and that with incredible manœuvrability, beaks agape as they gorged themselves. Soon the swallows would be gone, thought Yeoman, and once again England would be the poorer for their passing. Of all birds, he loved them the most.

They went into the inn and entered a long, low bar, its ceiling blackened by many years of tobacco smoke. Sunbeams like searchlights penetrated through the small windows, forming pools of light among the shadows, and it was some seconds before Yeoman's eyes accepted the sharp contrast. Then, as he and Julia moved towards the bar, he saw that there were several people in the room, seated around a heavy oak table near one of the windows, engrossed in a game of dominoes. One of them got up and opened a flap in the bar counter, passed through and approached the pilot, smiling. His face was round and red, capped by a tonsure of white hair, and his girth was considerable. He looked for all the world like an ageing Friar Tuck, and Yeoman liked him immediately.

'Good evening, sir,' the landlord said. 'And to you, miss. What can I get you?'

Yeoman smiled back at him. 'Good evening. A pint of bitter would be very nice.' He turned to Julia. 'What about you, love? A small bottle of beer, perhaps?'

She laughed. 'Not on your life! You drink pints, I drink pints! Bitter, please,' she told the landlord. He looked at her with considerable respect.

'It'll be the first time a woman's had a pint in this pub,' he said. 'You're American, miss, aren't you?'

Julia admitted that she was. The landlord nodded, as though that explained everything. 'Right-o, then,' he said with a wink. 'Two pints of bitter it is. I'll be back in a jiffy.'

He disappeared into a back room and returned half a minute later with a foaming pint mug in each hand. 'There you are,' he said, beaming. 'That's a drop of the good stuff.' Yeoman put his hand in his pocket, searching for some money, but the landlord shook his head, eyeing the pilot's wings and the medal ribbons under them. 'No, lad,' he said, 'the drinks are on the house. My own boy is in the Air Force. An air gunner.'

'How about one for us then, Joe?' asked one of the landlord's table companions, chuckling. The speaker was a wizened, ancient man dressed in waistcoat and corduroy trousers, a peaked cap pulled well down over his eyes. A clay pipe protruded from beneath it, exuding pungent smoke.

'Get away with you, Henry Boulter,' said Joe. 'You'd scrounge anything, you would.'

The old man grunted, peering at Yeoman and Julia. 'Don't stand there, you young 'uns,' he said. 'You make the room look untidy. Come over and sit yourselves down.'

'Thanks,' Yeoman said, 'but we don't want to interrupt your game.'

The old man removed his pipe and scratched his nose with the stem.

'Game's over, anyway,' he said. 'I'm not playing with him no more.' He pointed his pipe stem at Joe, the landlord. 'Bad loser, he is. Won't stand a pint for the winner.'

Yeoman laughed. 'All right, then. Just as long as we're not intruding.'

They sat down at the table and Yeoman brought out his own pipe and tobacco pouch, nodding to the others in greeting. They were all fairly elderly countrymen, and he guessed that this was their ritual at the end of their day's labour.

Henry looked from Yeoman to the tobacco pouch, then suddenly stretched out a hand and pushed it aside.

'Put it away, lad,' he said. 'Have some o' this instead. It'll do your insides the power of good.'

He produced a battered tin and offered it to Yeoman. The pilot prised off the lid and inspected the contents dubiously. Inside was a dark, rather stringy mixture that looked like chopped-up seaweed. Yeoman sniffed it tentatively and found that its aroma was unlike that of any tobacco he had encountered; it smelled of grass and wild herbs and garden mould.

'Go on, lad,' urged Henry. 'It won't bite.'

Yeoman realized that there were broad grins on the faces of the other men around the table and sensed that he was being taken for a ride, but he made up his mind to play along and filled his pipe to the brim, raising a rueful eyebrow at Julia. Henry snatched back his tin rather rudely.

'Hey, steady on there,' he said, winking at his companions. 'That stuff doesn't grow on trees, you know.'

Yeoman lit up and took an experimental puff, exhaling the smoke slowly. Very carefully, he placed his pipe on the table and sat gazing into space for a moment. Then his eyes began to water and beads of perspiration broke out on his brow. He grasped his pint mug with both hands and raised it to his lips, draining it in one long swallow. He set it down on the table with a bang and released his breath in a series of explosive gasps.

'Great God Almighty,' he croaked in a strangled voice. 'What was *that*?'

Beside him, old Henry and his cronies, and Julia too, were convulsed with laughter.

'Coltsfoot,' Henry said, spluttering with merriment.

'Coltsfoot? You mean the bloody *weed*? The yellow stuff that grows by the roadside?'

'Aye,' chortled Henry, nodding vigorously. 'I've smoked it since I was a lad your age, and it's never done me any harm. Go on—have another try at it.'

95

'No thanks,' Yeoman said firmly. 'I'll smoke my own, if you don't mind.'

'I'll have that back, then,' said Henry, eyeing the barely-touched contents of Yeoman's pipe. The pilot scraped the mixture out of the bowl into Henry's tin, then ordered another pint.

'Where are you from, lad?' asked Henry.

'Now then, Henry,' one of the old man's companions admonished. 'You should know better than to ask questions like that. Careless talk costs lives, you know.'

'Don't be bloody daft,' Henry snapped. 'Do I look like a German spy?'

'How would I know?' the other retorted. 'I've never seen one.'

'Oh, they go around dressed in long black cloaks, with floppy hats pulled down over their eyes and a cannonball under an arm with "bomb" written on it,' Julia said. The others laughed.

'Or dressed as nuns,' said one of the men at the table, who had not spoken until now. 'My lad was at Dunkirk, and he said they used to parachute 'em behind the lines, dressed up as nuns.'

'Did he actually come across any?' Yeoman asked, out of curiosity.

'No,' the man admitted. 'He just heard stories, that's all.'

'So did I,' said the pilot. 'I was in France too, during the retreat, and there were all sorts of wild rumours flying about.'

'According to my lad, they didn't see much of the Air Force at Dunkirk,' the man said cynically.

'Oh, we were there, all right,' Yeoman emphasized. He went on to explain how, fighting against enormous odds, the RAF's depleted fighter and bomber squadrons, together with their French allies, had striven to stem the German advance through Flanders and northern France; how Fighter Command, operating from bases in southern England, had torn great gaps in the ranks of the Luftwaffe over Dunkirk in air battles that were mostly invisible to the battered, weary troops on the bomb-swept beaches.

From time to time Julia added her own comments, for she had seen it all too, as a war correspondent attached to the French Army on the Maginot Line. The men listened intently, although Yeoman thought that he detected a certain scepticism in their attitude. And, he thought, who could blame them? Thousands of soldiers had come back from Dunkirk with a bitter feeling that they had been let down by the RAF, and Fighter Command's latest victory above England in that tumultuous summer of 1940 had, to some degree, been diminished by subsequent defeats in the Balkans and the Far East. Some day, perhaps, someone would set the record straight, but in the meantime it was galling to have to listen to constant rumblings of criticism.

After a short pause, Joe, the landlord, said: 'Well, we're giving it back to the buggers now, and no mistake. Look at this.' He picked up a copy of a local newspaper from the bar counter and quoted the headlines; '"RAF Pound Berlin. Over One Thousand Tons of Bombs Dropped." We're knocking hell out of 'em, I reckon, what with Sicily being captured and all.'

'And the Russians,' someone said. 'Don't forget the Russians. It said on the news this morning that they'd launched a big attack somewhere. I can't remember where. That's the trouble with all them funny Russian names, you can never remember 'em.'

'Just like the French,' Henry commented. 'Can't make head nor tail of 'em. That old Vichy must be a funny bugger, though,' he added thoughtfully.

The remark brought a roar of laughter from his companions. 'It's not a person, you daft old devil,' said Joe. 'It's a town in France, where they have their government.'

Henry gave an unconvinced grunt. 'Anyway,' he said, 'I'm fed up with all this war talk. Can't get away from it, not even at home. The missus sits glued to the wireless, listening to every news bulletin. Not that it makes much difference; there's nowt else on anyway. Bloody BBC's gone daft. Have you seen what's on tonight? *Welsh Half Hour*. I ask you! And then Tommy bloody Handley again, and after

97

that Russian piano music. I tell you,' he concluded bitterly, 'I wish I'd never bought the damned thing.'

The conversation drifted on aimlessly, turning eventually to farming. Yeoman bought a round of drinks, then he and Julia went outside and sat on a bench for a while, enjoying the sun while it lasted. A small boy, wearing outsize boots, a ragged shirt and a pair of short trousers with a gaping hole where the seat should have been, came and stared at them curiously for a while, his eyes unblinking and his thumb firmly inserted into his mouth. Yeoman had seen that same ragged look, that same state, a hundred times before, in France, North Africa and Malta; the colour of the skin and the style of dress might be different, but the stare was the same. It said, 'This is my territory, and you are strangers, intruding into it. I can be persuaded to go away, but only at a price.'

Julia made an unsuccessful attempt to find out the little boy's name, reaching out to take his hand, but he took a quick step backwards, just out of reach, continuing his vigil. By this time, Yeoman was beginning to feel faintly embarrassed. He fished in his pocket and brought out a penny, extending it to the child in the palm of his hand.

The boy seized it, removed his thumb for a fraction of a second, stuck out his tongue to its furthest extent and fled. Yeoman and Julia burst out laughing.

'That's what we're fighting for,' the pilot grinned. 'The future of Britain.'

'Not just of Britain,' his companion said, more seriously. 'There are millions of kids like that all over the world, most of them far worse off because of what we've done to them, George, our generation and the one before it. What's going to happen to them? What sort of people are they going to turn out to be?'

Yeoman made no reply for a few seconds. Then he said: 'People like you and me, I suppose. After all, wars have been happening for thousands of years, and after each one a new generation of children grows up and forgets. It's a pity that they do forget, because if they remembered what it was really like there wouldn't be any more wars. My dad used to talk about the last war a lot, when he was in the mood, but I could never grasp what it must really have been like. All I know is that when I was little my pals and I used to play English and Germans, and that nobody liked being the Germans because they were the ones who always got shot. I'd like to bet, too, that thirty years after this lot is over kids will still be playing English and Germans, assuming, that is, that we haven't fought anybody else in the meantime.'

The sound of singing came to them, breaking off their conversation. The noise swelled and now they could hear that it was a marching song, deep and with a swing to it that was unlike British marching songs.

A company of soldiers came round the corner, marching in column of route in full field kit, the tramp of their boots echoing rhythmically from the walls of the cottages. Children came running out to watch the khaki-clad ranks as they swung past along the village's solitary street.

The little boy to whom Yeoman had given a penny came running forward, stopped just by the roadside, pointed a finger at one of the soldiers and said, 'Bang!' The soldier made as though to unsling his rifle, scowling fiercely, and the child fled as fast as his outsize boots would let him, wailing in terror. A roar of laughter echoed down the marching column, changing to whistles and catcalls as the troops caught sight of Julia. The soldiers were quickly brought to order by an officer, who rapped out a sharp command and then flung up a salute, aimed at Julia rather than at Yeoman. The latter, who had been sitting bareheaded in the sun, waved in acknowledgement and called out *'Dobry wieczor!'*, for he had seen the 'Poland' shoulder flashes on the soldiers' uniforms. The officer, a captain, looked faintly surprised, then grinned hugely and returned the greeting. The column marched on and was soon lost to sight beyond the curve of the road.

'That was very accomplished of you, darling,' said Julia. Yeoman grinned and tried to assume a superior expression, examining his fingernails.

'Just one of my many talents,' he said. 'As a matter of

fact, I picked up quite a bit of the language when I was flying with the Polish squadron back in September '40.'

'Just so long as that's all you picked up,' she said, laughingly. 'Those Poles have quite a reputation for the fleshpots, or so I've been led to believe.'

He looked at her wickedly. 'Well,' he said, 'I remember spending quite a few fascinating nights with one particular red-headed seductress who told me a pack of lies about being an American war correspondent. I was completely innocent until I met her,' he laughed, dodging a playful swipe of her hand.

She leaned across and nibbled his ear, quite oblivious of the fact that the small boy, having overcome his fear of being massacred by Polish troops, had returned and was once again watching them, thumb in position.

'Are you going to seduce me tonight, darling?' she asked softly.

'Actually,' he replied unromantically, 'what I had more in mind was rape. You know my animal instincts. We'll have to preserve a bit of decorum, though, and put you in the spare bedroom, because Father's a bit of an old-fashioned type. The spare bedroom, however, happens to be right next to mine, Father is a very heavy sleeper and the floorboards on the landing don't creak.'

He looked at his watch and then took her hand, rising from the bench. 'Time we were on our way,' he said, smiling down at her. 'I'm suddenly very hungry, and some of Dad's cold roast beef and pickles would be just the ticket. That's one advantage of living in the country; not many people go hungry.'

They went back into the inn for a moment, to say goodbye to the others, and then drove off on the last lap of their journey. Julia let her hand rest lightly on Yeoman's knee and gave it a little squeeze from time to time, half absent-mindedly. They spoke little, each being busy with private thoughts.

Yeoman, roused by the proximity of Julia's body, anticipating their lovemaking, nevertheless felt a strange sadness. The sight of the Poles had brought back many memories of those savage, glorious days of three years ago, a span of time that seemed like an eternity now, when men from every corner of Occupied Europe, the Americas and the Commonwealth had fought and died over the harvest-fields of Kent and elsewhere in the embattled island; men who had fought for an ideal, because they had loved flying and adventure and because they were young, or because—like many of the Poles—they had bitter personal scores to settle.

The names came flooding back into his mind. Adamek... Bronsky, killed in his exploding Hurricane on the edge of the stratosphere... young Hamilton, shot down on his first operation... Fred Kirby, falling in flames, trapped in his cockpit... Simon Wynne-Williams, also spinning down in flames, to survive with terrible burns... Jim Callender, the born survivor, who had become Yeoman's close friend; an American, he had later transferred to the USAAF and was now commanding a group of P-47 Thunderbolts in Suffolk... Mervyn Kendal, who had commanded the Polish squadron to which Yeoman had belonged; they had fought together again, in the Western Desert and Crete, and Kendal was now commanding a fighter tactics school up in Northumberland... the list was endless, the names marching across his mind in endless procession. There had been others, too, good friends who had given their lives in the terrible cauldron over Malta: Gerry Powell... Kearney... McCallum... he closed his mind with an effort, knowing that he would never forget them, but that now was not the time to remember them. One day, if he lived, his pen would capture them all, expanding the scribbled words in the crumpled, tea-stained notebooks he always carried with him, telling a future world, a world in which small children with ragged trousers were grown into men, of the lost generation and the sacrifices it had made.

Beside him, Julia's face was turned away, and he could not see that her eyes were filled with tears. Mistily, she watched the greens and golds of the English landscape flow past, looking quickly back from time to time as she caught sight of cows, grazing placidly beyond some gap in the hedgerows. It was as though she wished to capture every tranquil scene as it flicked past, like an individual frame from a film, and lock it in her mind forever.

And much later, in John Yeoman's house, long after the old man had gone to bed and she lay beside his son, who slept a sleep of exhausted contentment, she buried her face in her pillow and wept, quietly so that her sobs would not waken him. She wept because there was so little time, and because despite all her avowals, she knew that she might never see him again; her luck could not last much longer.

For within a week, unknown to all except herself and a handful of people within a very clandestine organization known as Special Operations Executive, Julia Connors, alias Madeleine Lefèvre, would parachute into Occupied France for the second time in six months.

Chapter Seven

ONE MORNING IN SEPTEMBER, WITH A THUNDERCLAP OF EN-
gines, the twelve Mosquitos of No. 373 Squadron, the unit
which was to share Burningham with No. 380, arrived overhead and broke into the circuit, landing to the accompaniment
of comments from the few observers who had bothered to
turn out and watch the new arrivals.

"About bloody time, too. Took their time getting
here...Jesus, that was a ropey landing...' A Mosquito
bounced high as its wheels hit the tarmac and went round
again, both engines roaring. 'Bloody amateur...weird-look-
ing bastards, aren't they?'

The new Mosquitos—Mk XIIs, as the watchers from 380
Squadron later learned—were certainly sinister in appearance. They were painted black all over, and the white had
been removed from the roundels and the fin flashes. Peering
closely at them as they taxied past, the 380 Squadron men
observed that the new arrivals had no machine-guns, and
guessed that the space normally occupied by the latter must
now house some form of airborne interception radar. The
four cannon under the nose, however, were retained. There
were also some odd-looking aerials sticking out of the wings,
which no one could identify.

The black-painted Mosquitos trundled off across the airfield to their dispersals on the far side, and a coach set out to pick up their crews. There were no operations that day, so those crews of 380 Squadron who were not flying or engaged on some other duty gathered in their respective messes to meet the newcomers.

The commanding officer of No. 373 Squadron, Squadron Leader Clive Bowen, was a big, soft-spoken Welshman who had been well on his way towards playing Rugby at international level before the war intervened. Although Yeoman had never met him, he learned that Bowen had also been in Malta at the same time as himself, flying Beaufighter night fighters from the bomb-torn island. He and his radar observer, Flying Officer Alan Wells, had eight kills to their credit while working as a team, all of them scored at night.

Yeoman and Bowen commandeered a corner of the bar in the officers' mess and fell to reminiscing. Yeoman did not normally drink before lunch, but this was a special occasion and, in any case, the dice were absent. If operations were on, a pair of dice would be placed on the mantelpiece, conspicuous for all to see. It was an old custom dating back to the days of the Royal Flying Corps, and it had given rise to the RAF slang exressions 'We're dicing tonight' and 'It looks a bit dicey'.

After lunch, Bowen took Yeoman out to have a look at one of 373 Squadron's Mosquitos, explaining its electronic equipment. He told Yeoman that the delay in bringing the squadron to full operational status had been caused by a sudden change in the airborne interception equipment; the Mosquitos had originally been fitted with Mk VIII AI, but then someone in Air Ministry had decided that this was too secret to be used on operations over enemy territory and so it had been replaced by the earlier Mk IV set. The Mosquitos were also fitted with another piece of equipment, code-named 'Serrate'. This device permitted the radar observer to home on to enemy night fighter transmissions from as much as a hundred miles away and the information received was displayed on the AI cathode ray tubes, the observer switching from one set to the other as required. Since 'Serrate' only gave a target's bearing, and not its range, AI was used as the fighter closed in to the attack.

Yeoman learned that the combination of Mk IV AI and 'Serrate' had already been used experimentally by the Beaufighters of No. 141 Squadron, which had carried out a series of intruder and bomber support operations between the middle of June and the first days of September, destroying thirteen enemy aircraft.

'Well,' said Yeoman, as they drove back towards the airfield buildings, 'it looks as though we'll really be able to get stuck into them now.'

'Yes,' Bowen agreed, 'but it's a matter of keeping one step ahead, especially in this radar business. The Beaufighter boys reported that, towards the end of their trial "Serrate" operations, their Mk IV AI was being jammed in a fairly limited way, so it seems that the Germans are catching on to our weaknesses. We don't yet know how effective the Hun jamming is now, but I've no doubt we will in a few days' time after we've carried out our first "Mahmoud" operation.'

'"Mahmoud"?' Yeoman looked at his companion questioningly.

'That's the code-name they've allocated to our night bomber support operations,' Bowen explained. 'We'll either be flying alongside the bomber stream, out on the flanks, or hanging around over the German night fighter assembly beacons to see if we can find a bit of trade.'

'Rather you than us,' Yeoman grinned. 'It doesn't sound too healthy to me.'

Bowen grinned back to him. 'About as healthy as low-level attacks on enemy airfields in daylight,' he said. 'Still, I suppose it's a matter of what you're used to. Personally, I've done so much night flying that I just don't feel right unless there's someone beside me, telling me where to go all the time.'

They pulled up outside the mess and made for the entrance, intending to read the newspapers until teatime, but Yeoman's anticipation of a tranquil afternoon was rudely shattered by the adjutant, who came trotting along the corridor and took him urgently by the arm.

'There you are,' he said breathlessly. 'I've been looking for you everywhere.' He lowered his voice. 'Bad news, I'm afraid. Flying Officer O'Grady has just tried to kill himself.'

'Christ!' Yeoman exclaimed. 'What happened?'

'Well,' Rees told him, 'it was all a bit strange. A few of us, including O'Grady, were sitting in the anteroom after lunch, reading the papers, when suddenly this navigator burst in and made straight for where O'Grady was sitting.' The adjutant looked at Bowen. 'The navigator was one of your chaps, sir, Flying Officer Cooper.

'Anyway, Cooper stood over O'Grady, who turned as white as a sheet when he saw him and started to get up. That was when Cooper hit him and knocked him clean over the back of the chair. Then Cooper said, in a very loud voice so that we could all hear: "You stinking yellow bastard. I knew I'd catch up with you one day. That was for—" and he mentioned a name I didn't get. A man's name, I think.'

'Go on,' Yeoman prompted. 'What then? What did O'Grady do?'

'He just lay on the floor for a while—it must only have been a second or two, in reality, because the rest of us hardly had time to get on our feet—and then he scrambled up and dashed out of the room. Cooper just looked a bit sheepish, apologized to us, then sat down and hid himself behind a magazine.'

'Who saw Cooper hit O'Grady?' Yeoman wanted to know. Rees listed four or five people. 'Most of the officers had drifted off,' he said, 'and none of the mess staff were present, fortunately.'

Yeoman nodded. 'Right. And what next?'

'I asked Terry Saint if he would go and see if O'Grady was all right. After all, the man looked pretty shaken. He hadn't been gone more than a few seconds when we heard a shot, and then Saint came running back shouting to us to fetch the MO, because O'Grady was lying in his room with his head in a pool of blood. He had apparently tried to put a bullet through his brain, but messed things up and only grazed his skull. He's in sick quarters now.'

'I'd better get over there right away, then,' Yeoman said, then turned to Bowen. 'Clive, would you mind getting hold of this Cooper chap and finding out his side of the story? He seems to have precipitated something that's going to take a bit of sorting out.' Bowen nodded and turned away, then asked the adjutant if he had informed anyone else about the incident.

'Not yet,' Rees admitted. 'There hasn't really been time.'

'Then do me a favour and don't,' Yeoman said, 'at least not for the time being. I want to talk to O'Grady first, and get to the bottom of all this. It's not as if the chap is badly hurt, or as if someone tried to murder him. Maybe we can smooth it all over.'

The adjutant smiled thinly. 'I'm all in favour of that, sir,' he said, and gave the pilot a knowing look. 'I don't want to spend the next few days writing reports, either.' Yeoman gazed at him for a couple of seconds, then nodded. They understood one another.

'Don't stay too long, George. He's still a bit shaken up.' Squadron Leader Fraser, the Medical Officer, closed the door behind Yeoman and the latter heard his footsteps receding down the corridor.

O'Grady was lying full length on the bed. Apart from his jacket, collar and tie, he was still fully clothed. There was a bandage around his head. As Yeoman walked towards him, he turned his face to the wall.

'Look at me, O'Grady,' Yeoman said quietly. Reluctantly, O'Grady's head moved around, although he avoided his squadron commander's eyes. He looked pale and miserable.

Yeoman pulled up a chair and sat astride it, his arms resting on the back, looking down at the man on the bed.

'Now then, O'Grady,' he said, 'the Doc assures me that you are going to be all right, so I am not going to treat you like some sort of invalid. I want to know what connection there is between you and Flying Officer Cooper, and why you tried to do away with yourself. Now I'm no bloody psychiatrist and I haven't got all day. All I know is that at this moment I am looking at a pilot in my squadron who is in some sort of trouble, and I want to know why. So start talking.'

'What will happen to me, sir?' The voice was pitiful, almost whining. O'Grady seemed on the verge of tears. Yeoman felt a sudden wave of sympathy for the man, sensing his inner torment, then brushed aside the sentiment and said brusquely: 'I'll be better placed to tell you that when I've heard your story. So come on, man, pull yourself together.'

O'Grady brushed a trembling hand across his eyes. Then, staring up at the ceiling, he murmured, so quietly that Yeoman had to lean forward to hear him:

'It's been a nightmare. Day and night, for nearly two years now. You see, sir, I killed a man.'

There was a pause, and Yeoman said, 'Well, most of us have done that. What's so different about your case?'

'It happened just after I'd gone on to Whirlwinds,' O'Grady continued, almost as though he were talking to himself. 'I was flying number two to my flight commander on a ranger over France. There were just the two of us. Our brief was to shoot up trains in the Pas de Calais area.' He fell silent for a few moments, and Yeoman prompted him to go on.

'We found a train and attacked it. It must have been pretty important, because it was stiff with light flak. I was scared stiff—it was the first time anyone had shot at me. I mean, I was literally frozen with terror.'

The words were coming more easily now, tumbling over themselves as O'Grady strove to unburden himself. 'The flight commander called for a second attack, and he went in first. It was then I saw the fighters, coming down hard from above.'

For the first time, his eyes fixed directly on Yeoman. 'I tried to warn the flight commander, sir, honestly I did,' he said pathetically, 'but I was so terrified I couldn't speak. I don't know what made me do it, but I...I just turned the

Whirlwind round and headed for the Channel flat out, away from the Messerschmitts.

'I got back to base, told them the flight commander had been shot down, as I was pretty certain he must have been, and that I had got away by the skin of my teeth. Then I waited around in agony for the next hour, waiting to see if he came back after all.' O'Grady's voice choked, and his hand went to his eyes again.

'Oh, God,' he whispered, 'I prayed for him not to come back. I was overjoyed when he didn't. The day we heard via the usual channels that he had in fact been shot down and killed, I went out and got drunk. And I thought that was the end of the matter, that no one would ever know what a coward I'd been.'

A stifled sob broke from him. 'I was wrong,' he said hoarsely. 'Oh, Christ, how wrong I was! The guilt came after that, you see. It would hit me suddenly, at all times of the day and night. I couldn't sleep, couldn't eat. The other chaps on the squadron began to notice it and make comments . . . I began to avoid them as much as possible. On operations, I started taking all sorts of stupid risks, half hoping that I'd be killed too.'

He gave a sudden, strange laugh. 'I was even recommended for a DFC, once,' he said. 'Can you imagine that? Anyway, I didn't get it.'

He reached out for a glass of water on the bedside cabinet and took a long drink before going on with his story.

'Things went from bad to worse. I started having nightmares, horrible dreams in which I saw the flight commander's face, torn and burnt, grinning at me. I started drinking more, too.'

Yeoman made no comment. Privately, he wondered why O'Grady had not been taken off operations a long time ago. The signs of an impending mental breakdown were all too apparent.

'There was a party one night,' O'Grady went on dully. 'I got tight, confided in someone, another Air Force type who was a complete stranger. He was very sympathetic. What I

109

didn't know at the time was that he was a friend of my flight commander's brother.'

'Who, I would guess, was Flying Officer Cooper,' Yeoman interjected. The other nodded miserably.

'That's right. He was overseas at the time, but this other chap must have written to him, because after a while the letters started arriving. Cooper swore to expose me for what I really was, a coward. Someone who had turned tail and left another man to die. I can imagine how he gloated,' O'Grady said bitterly, 'when he found out I was here. He must have asked someone to point me out.'

Once again, Yeoman was on the receiving end of O'Grady's pathetic, pleading look. 'What's going to happen to me, sir?' the man asked again. 'I won't be taken off operations, will I?'

'That's not just for me to decide, O'Grady. However, I do know that you need a rest. I'm going to leave you now, so I want you just to lie there and take things easy for a while.'

Now that he knew O'Grady's full story, he felt a certain compassion for him. The man had clearly been on the verge of cracking up for some time, and to carry on under those circumstances must have required a considerable amount of courage. O'Grady was no coward, and it needed someone to tell him so. Nevertheless, the man's operational flying days were over.

'Sir!' O'Grady called out suddenly, as Yeoman went to the door. The squadron commander turned towards him.

'My mother won't have to know about this, will she? I mean, it would just about finish her. She only wanted me to do well—to make a name for myself.'

Yeoman had taken the trouble to look up O'Grady's personal file in considerable detail, and to make discreet inquiries about the man as soon as he had realized that O'Grady was plagued by some deep-rooted internal problem. He knew that his mother was a widow, eking out a living in a little corner shop in some Liverpool back street. She must have been terribly proud of her son, a commissioned officer.

'No,' Yeoman said. 'Don't worry about that. You'll be all right in a day or two; there's no need for anyone to inform your next of kin.' He grinned suddenly. 'If that bullet had gone a quarter of an inch the other way we'd have had to, though. So don't try anything as stupid as that again.'

O'Grady shook his head. 'No,' he said, 'I won't. Thank you, sir. Thanks a lot.'

Yeoman closed the door behind him and leaned against it for a moment, sighing. Life as a squadron commander seemed full of complexities, hardly any of them to do with operational flying. Still, he thought philosophically, that's what I'm paid for. He shrugged his shoulders and went in search of the MO.

Fraser looked quizzically at Yeoman as the latter entered his office.

'Well, George,' he said. 'what do you think, an LMF case?' Yeoman shook his head. Lack of moral fibre, the rather cruel expression used at the time to describe aircrew whose nervous state no longer permitted them to fly operationally, did not fit O'Grady's particular case.

'No, Doc, in a strange sort of way he's got plenty of guts. He doesn't want to be taken off operations; quite the contrary. In fact, deep down inside him the poor bugger wants to get himself killed.' Briefly, he outlined O'Grady's story.

Fraser sucked at the stem of his unlit pipe, nodding slowly. 'All right,' he said, 'I'll arrange for him to have the full works—psychiatric treatment, the lot. I'll keep him here for a few days, though, before having him moved. He sounds an interesting case, and I've often fancied myself as something of an amateur head-shrinker. I'd like to try out a few ideas of my own on him.'

'God help him,' Yeoman grinned, and left. Mentally, he ticked off the things he had to do. The Station Commander was away and would not be back until tomorrow, so until then matters rested very much in Yeoman's own hands. There would have to be an enquiry, of course, but Yeoman was confident that Group Captain Davison would share his own point of view and not allow things to get out of hand. Nothing was worse for the morale of a unit, he thought, than an incident of this kind.

Yeoman suddenly swore fluently, not so much at O'Grady as at himself, for allowing the incident to happen. He should have concentrated more on O'Grady weeks ago, should have taken greater pains to lay bare the man's trouble, and if necessary to have him removed from the unit.

George, he told himself angrily, you might be a reasonable pilot, but you've still got a hell of a lot to learn about command.

Chapter Eight

A FORTNIGHT LATER, AS THE TEMPO OF AIR OPERATIONS IN-creased, the O'Grady incident had been virtually forgotten. The unfortunate man had been quietly spirited away from the airfield and a new pilot, Flying Officer Collins, posted in as a replacement. The two Burningham squadrons were now given Wing status and a Wing Commander arrived to take overall command, relieving Yeoman of some of the more onerous duties. The new man's name was Rothbury, and Yeoman learned that he had pioneered a number of long-range routes across the more inaccessible parts of the British Empire before the war, flying Vickers Wellesley monoplanes. Later, in Blenheims, he had fought the Japanese in Burma during the long retreat back to the Indian frontier. The ribbons of the DSO and the DFC were evidence of his courage.

Rothbury brought with him an infectious enthusiasm which, added to the morale-building process already started by Yeoman, soon manifested itself in a growing success rate for the Burningham squadrons. The crews of No. 373, ranging far out over darkened Europe, scored their first kills against the enemy night fighters, while No. 380 began a series of intensive dawn and dusk attacks on fighter airfields around the German defensive perimeter, from Cherbourg to Denmark. Remarkably, although some Mosquitos returned from

113

these operations with varying degrees of damage, there were no losses during this period.

The situation, however, was not to last.

The pilots of Fighter Wing 301 had been waiting for just such an opportunity for a long time. Ever since the middle of August, Richter had been pressing his superiors for permission to use his small force of single-engined fighters on fast intruder operations against airfields in England. He had spent hours planning such operations with meticulous care, and had submitted one scheme after another only to have it rejected by higher authority.

The Führer, it seemed, had a long-standing aversion to intruder operations, and in fact had forbidden them altogether as long ago as the end of 1941. It had taken him eighteen months to relent, and even then intruder operations over the British Isles were mere pinpricks, reduced for the most part to sorties by single aircraft, usually Junkers 88s or Dornier 217s. Losses had been high of late, for the British were using new and improved airborne detection equipment, fitted to their latest Mosquito night fighters.

The solution, Richter was convinced, was to strike hard with a large force of intruders, say thirty or forty aircraft, at sunset. The force would be split into three waves: the first to attack a selected USAAF bomber base, the second an RAF heavy bomber airfield, and the third to strike at the nerve-centre of the RAF's own intruder operations.

The latter was now known to Luftwaffe Intelligence. It was the airfield at Burningham, in Norfolk, and whatever happened, Richter was determined to lead an attack on it in person. At the beginning of October, therefore, Richter had submitted a revised plan to the Luftwaffe High Command via his immediate superiors, envisaging a strike against Burningham by Focke-Wulf 190s fitted with long-range tanks and probably operating from an advanced airfield in Holland. The choice of sunset for all three strikes was dictated by the need to catch as many British and American aircraft as possible on the ground; ideally, it would take place in the wake

114

of an American daylight raid, which was almost certain to be followed by an RAF night attack. The prospect of catching a couple of squadrons of Lancasters or Halifaxes as they prepared to take off, with full loads of fuel and bombs, was a juicy one indeed.

To Richter's astonishment, the plan had finally been returned with an 'approved' stamp on it, and he had lost no time in setting about organizing the operation. Obtaining approval for the temporary withdrawal of Fighter Wing 301 from defensive operations had proved another obstacle, but he had surmounted it in the end and had obtained authority to station the Wing's three squadrons at Gilze Rijen, in Holland, to await a suitable moment.

It came on 14 October, at the end of a hectic week during which the Americans had attacked Bremen, Marienburg, Danzig and Münster. Now, on the fourteenth, they once again made the long haul to Schweinfurt with 280 bombers, and suffered appalling losses.

For Richter's pilots, it was galling to have to remain on the ground, their fighters in specially-prepared camouflaged revetments round the airfield perimeter as an insurance against strafing Allied fighters, while other Luftwaffe units joined the battle all along the bombers' route. Once again, as they would learn later, sixty heavy bombers fell to the fighters and the flak.

At last, just before five o'clock in the afternoon, Richter and twenty-six other pilots climbed into the cockpits of the Focke-Wulfs. A few minutes later, while half a dozen Messerschmitt 109s circled the airfield as a precaution against marauding enemy fighters, they roared down the runway in sections of three and raced at low level towards the Dutch coast, forming up into three compact groups of nine aircraft as they did so.

Ahead of them, the sun was an outsize red ball on the western horizon, cut in half by a thin line of cloud. They pointed their noses directly towards it. On either side, the chill autumnal sky, criss-crossed by the drifting remnants of a few vapour trails, merged with a steel-grey sea. Although the FW 190's cockpit was warm and the big BMW 801 radial engine roared smoothly, Richter gave an involuntary shudder, a product of the single-engine fighter pilot's inbred dislike of flying over long stretches of water.

The other 190s were packed around him like a shoal of blunt-nosed predatory fish. Richter noted with satisfaction that the fighters' mottled grey-blue upper surfaces blended in nicely with the sea; it would take a keen-eyed enemy pilot to spot them from higher up.

Richter rocked his wings as the Norfolk coastline appeared ahead and the three groups of fighters spread out, ready to break off towards their assigned targets. Richter had deliberately picked three that were grouped fairly closely together, so that the Focke-Wulfs would be able to support each other, if necessary, on the way out. They carried no bombs, but their built-in armament of four 20-mm cannon and two 13-mm machine-guns should be sufficient to cause considerable damage to soft-skinned targets, and it was aircraft they sought rather than airfield installations.

They thundered over the coast between Lowestoft and Great Yarmouth, and immediately afterwards the nine aircraft led by Johnny Schumacher curved away to the south, following the railway line that would lead them to their objective, the American bomber base of Mullingworth, just inside Suffolk. Ninety seconds later the second group also broke away; their target was the RAF station at South Metterton and its adjacent satellite aerodrome, where three squadrons of Halifaxes were based.

Richter led his nine Focke-Wulfs straight on, spearing over roads, railways and water courses. He had studied maps of this area for so long that he knew the terrain by heart; his group of fighters was no more than half a mile off their intended track, and Burningham was less than three minutes away.

The three waves of fighters hit their respective targets with only seconds to spare between them. Johnny Schumacher's formation was the first to attack, bearing down on Mullingworth at full throttle. Mullingworth was the home of two groups of B-24 Liberators, and as they swept down on the airfield the jubilant German pilots saw that several of the huge bombers were still in the circuit, orbiting the field like great dark crows in the gathering dusk, wheels down and navigation lights blazing as they awaited their turn to land.

Schumacher closed in behind the great bulk of a B-24 which was approaching the runway and opened fire from point-blank range, seeing his shells burst with vivid flashes on the wings and fuselage. The bomber started to burn almost immediately, and a moment later it dived into the ground just short of the runway and exploded in gouts of blazing fuel. Schumacher swept over the wreck, ruddering to left and right as he sprayed the airfield with fire, then pulled up in a steep climb and looked back for another target.

Below him, two more Liberators were in flames as the other pilots made their attacks. In less than half a minute, the whole airfield was lit up by the bombers' funeral pyres. Another Liberator, harassed by a Focke-Wulf, managed to get down on the runway, but burst into flames as soon as its wheels touched and slewed on to the grass, spewing débris as its undercarriage collapsed.

The airfield defences were now adding to the confusion, spewing multicoloured tracers in all directions. As he circled the field, Schumacher noted with satisfaction one bomber, pulverized by American shells, plunging into the runway intersection. Arrowing down at high speed through the lurid smoke, he lined up with the squat control tower and fired a long burst into it, seeing two dark figures hurl themselves from the balcony as he swept past.

The ground fire was growing in intensity. He drew off to one side, counting the other Focke-Wulfs as they popped up out of the drifting smoke at the end of their second strafing run; they were all there, looking like orange bullets as their wings reflected the spreading fires below. He ordered them to set course for home and they sped away to the east, leaving behind the blazing wrecks of six Liberators.

The second wave of fighters, bearing down on South Metterton, enjoyed less good fortune, for the airfield was deserted. Unknown to the Germans, the Halifaxes had moved to northern Scotland that very morning to take part in an attack on enemy installations in Norway. Only two Halifaxes remained, together with a Lancaster which had landed there earlier in the day with engine trouble; all three were quickly knocked out, but one of the German pilots misjudged his strafing run in the dusk and flew straight into the ground, scattering pieces of himself and his aircraft in a long trail beside the main runway.

It was a different story at Burningham. Here, all but two of the Mosquitos—both of them 373 Squadron aircraft— were on the ground. All of 373's crews with the exception of the missing pair—who had been scrambled only minutes earlier to intercept an unidentified aircraft to the north—were in the main briefing room, preparing for the night's operations, while those of 380 Squadron were in their messes, tucking into bacon and eggs after a day of intensive flying. In the morning, at the request of Coastal Command, who were tied up elsewhere, they had attacked two big flak ships off the Schelde Estuary, a dangerous and hair-raising task which had been accomplished without loss, although Romilly had brought his aircraft back on one engine, and in the afternoon they had once again carried out daylight bomber support operations over Belgium. There had been a short dogfight in which Reed had destroyed a Messerschmitt 110, together with another probably destroyed, and two other pilots had each claimed a Messerschmitt 109 damaged.

Yeoman arrived late in the mess dining room and smiled at the pretty young WAAF who appeared at his elbow, bearing a tray of food. She picked up a plate and was about to set it down in front of him when there was a sudden snarl of aero-engines and the windows rattled to the bark of cannon-fire. The girl screamed and dropped the bacon and eggs in Yeoman's lap. Swearing, he jumped to his feet, brushed her aside and made for the door, closely followed by the others.

Belatedly, the airfield sirens began to wail.

'Quick,' Yeoman yelled at McManners, who was pounding along at his elbow. 'The car!'

They flung themselves into Yeoman's Morgan and roared off down the winding road towards the hangars. Personnel were streaming towards the airfield from all sides, on foot or on whatever transport they could grab. There was no thought of taking to the air-raid shelters.

The unmistakable square-cut silhouette of a Focke-Wulf 190 flashed overhead, so low that they could make out the big black crosses under its wings, even in the dusk. It disappeared behind one of the hangars and they heard the hammering of its guns. A second Focke-Wulf appeared, rocketing up towards the sky, dodging tracer. A series of terrific thumps shook the airfield and a dark cloud of smoke billowed up, its source as yet invisible.

Yeoman kept his foot on the accelerator and careered round the corner of a hangar, dodging groups of running airmen as he headed straight for the dispersals. The noise was terrific, the Bofors guns that were sited round the field adding their clamour to the scream of the Focke-Wulfs' engines and the clatter of their cannon. Shell splinters rattled on the hangar roofs and bounced lethally from the road surface.

Yeoman's only thought was to try and reach his Mosquitos, to make a desperate effort to get at least some of them into the air before they were wiped out, and confront Burningham's attackers. Then, as he rounded the hangars, the full enormity of the disaster hit him with stunning force.

At least four of 380 Squadron's Mosquitos were total wrecks, with greedy flames eating into their wooden structures. From the lakes of fuel that surrounded them, dense columns of acrid smoke rose into the evening sky. Smoke also rose from the far side of the field, where 373 Squadron's aircraft were parked.

The Morgan screeched to a stop and Yeoman leaped out, running like a madman towards his own aircraft, which still appeared to be undamaged. An instant later, McManners brought him down with a Rugby tackle that knocked all the wind from his body. He struggled to rise, but the flight commander held him down firmly.

The sound of thudding explosions was loud in his ears. There was a staccato cracking noise, all around, and the thunderclap roar of an engine. A Focke-Wulf swept over the two prone men, its slipstream plucking at them.

Cautiously, they raised their heads. The Mosquito towards which Yeoman had been running was shattered and smoking. An instant later, flames burgeoned from it. Behind them, the little Morgan lay on its side, its silver metal torn by cannon shells.

They picked themselves up shakily as the snarl of engines receded in the distance.

'Christ, boss,' McManners gasped. 'That was too bloody close for comfort!'

Yeoman fought to regain his breath. A waft of oily smoke caught at his throat, making him retch.

'Thanks, Mac,' he said. 'I reckon you saved my skin.' He looked around at the burning aircraft, ducking as ammunition began to explode with a series of vicious cracks. 'Lord, what an awful bloody mess! It looks as though the Huns got clean away, too.'

McManners pointed towards the centre of the airfield, past the wrecked Mosquitos. 'There's one bastard that didn't,' he said. Shielding his eyes against the glare of the flames, Yeoman made out the shattered wreck of an aircraft some distance away. There was not much left except an angular tail fin, jutting up from a mound of twisted metal, but it was enough to identify the crashed machine as an FW 190.

'Come on,' said Yeoman, raising his voice above the crackling of the flames and the shrilling of bells as fire engines and ambulances converged on the scene of carnage, 'let's take a closer look at the damage. It looks as if we've taken some casualties, too.'

They made their way to where some airmen were clustered around an inert form on the ground, close to one of the wrecked Mosquitos. Two medical orderlies ran up with a stretcher, bent over the casualty and then lifted him gently.

Yeoman pushed his way through the group of airmen. 'Come on, you lot,' he snapped, 'get weaving! There's a lot to be done.' Their faces were shocked, but his curt words had the desired effect and they dispersed quickly. Yeoman went forward and bent over the stetcher, felt his stomach turn sickeningly as he recognized the injured man. He glanced enquiringly at one of the orderlies, who shook his head slowly.

Warrant Officer Len Thomas opened his eyes, focused on Yeoman and smiled weakly. His lips moved, and the pilot bent forward to catch what he was trying to say.

'Just...just like France, sir.' He coughed, then suddenly stretched out a hand and clutched Yeoman's arm with surprising strength. 'My engines, sir,' he pleaded. 'Make them look after my engines.' His voice trailed away. He made a last effort to say something else, then blood came from his mouth and the light went from his eyes.

Yeoman stood up, dully watching the orderlies take the stretcher away. Then he turned and strode off into the lurid night, towards the heart of the chaos, hoping that no one would notice the tears glistening in his eyes.

The cost had been high. Five of no. 380 Squadron's Mosquitos had been totally destroyed—almost half the unit's complement—and so had three of No. 373's machines. In terms of human life, the cost had been six airmen killed and four wounded, one of them seriously. All of them were ground crew, who had been working on the aircraft at the time of the attack. The Germans had lost two Focke-Wulfs, one of which had crashed on the airfield and the other— intercepted purely by chance by one of the two 373 Squadron Mosquitos which had been in the air at the time—into the sea off Lowestoft. The remainder had got clean away.

Wing Commander Rothbury sat in his office and stared at a square of torn aluminium, salvaged from the crashed Focke-Wulf. There was a painted badge on it, partly blackened by fire, but still recognizable as a pair of slanting cat's eyes, yellow against a dark blue background.

Rothbury looked in turn at Yeoman and Bowen, then at the Intelligence Officer, Flight Lieutenant Freddie Barnes. It was four days since the raid, and the three officers were still subdued from attending the funerals of Warrant Officer Thomas and the airmen who had died. They lay together now, side by side, in the cemetery of the little village church down the road, with the body of the dead Focke-Wulf pilot close by.

'So, Freddie,' said Rothbury. 'You believe you've got something?'

'Yes, sir.' Barnes gave his habitual nervous cough, blinking furiously behind his glasses.

'The information came through from Air Ministry just a while ago. It's believed that the insignia'—he nodded towards the cat's eyes—'belongs to a new special duties Luftwaffe fighter unit, Jagdgeschwader 301. We don't have much on it, but we think it was formed last July or August for sort of freelance fighter operations. It moves about quite a lot, depending on where the action is.'

'Hm.' Rothbury removed his pipe. 'That doesn't tell us a lot, does it?'

'Well, sir,' Barnes continued, 'there's a little more. We think we know who the commanding officer is.' He opened a folder and took out a photostat copy of a page from the Swiss aviation magazine *Interavia*, handing it across the desk to the wing commander.

Rothbury looked down at the photograph of the enemy pilot, who wore an impressive number of decorations, and read the details out loud. The cutting was several months old.

'Captain Joachim Richter. Well, he's presumably had a bit of promotion since then. "Fighter hero returns from Sicily,"' he read. '"Captain Joachim Richter, veteran of the campaigns in France, the Balkans and Russia, has been awarded the Knight's Cross with Swords and Diamonds on his return to Germany after successfully completing a tour of operations in Sicily. According to the Luftwaffe High Command, Captain Richter has seventy-three victories to his credit, most of them scored on the Eastern Front. Captain Richter was reported to be a close friend of the legendary Major Werner Mölders, who was killed in an air accident in the winter of 1941."'

Rothbury handed the cutting to Yeoman. 'That's all there is,' he said, 'but it's enough. This chap sounds a pretty big

122

fish, and one who knows his business. If he's organizing a strong force of intruders for operations against our airfields, then we might well have a serious problem on our hands. What do you think, George?'

Yeoman made no reply. He was studying Richter's photograph, totally absorbed. In a strange way, he had the uncanny feeling that he was looking into a mirror, that he was staring at a reflection of himself, in different uniform. Then the feeling passed as he took note of the obvious facial differences, and he handed the cutting on to Bowen.

Nevertheless, he could not shake off an odd sense of *déjà vu*, as though somewhere, sometime, he had met this man face to face. But that, of course, was impossible.

'I think,' he said slowly, 'that we ought to give Herr Richter, and Jagdgeschwader 301, a good deal of our time.'

Chapter Nine

THE LONE MOSQUITO DRONED HIGH OVER NORTHERN FRANCE, heading deeper into enemy territory. Far below it stretched an unbroken sea of stratus, blotting out the darkened land.

'We're entering the patrol area now, skipper.'

At the controls, Clive Bowen smiled to himself. The tone of his navigator's voice was decisive; Alan Wells was never in any doubt, even when navigating by dead reckoning with never a sight of the ground. The Rhine would be below their nose now, with their objective, Spayer airfield, on its west bank.

Bowen throttled back and took the mosquito down to five thousand feet, following the series of courses given to him by Wells, quartering the sky around the hidden aerodrome. Once, briefly, the clouds parted to reveal a beacon, flashing morse, and they caught a glimpse of approach lights before the dark curtain rolled together once more.

They had been on patrol for ten minutes when Wells' crisp voice came over the intercom again. The navigator was glued to the dancing images on his cathode ray tubes, and now he tensed as a firm, clear echo manifested itself above the shimmering ground clutter.

'Contact dead ahead, crossing port to starboard, two and a half miles.'

Bowen opened the throttles and increased speed to 280 mph, swinging the Mosquito round on to a heading of zero-eight-zero degrees, slowly narrowing the distance as Wells continued to issue instructions. The target, still invisible to the naked eye, lost height until it was just above the cloud tops and began to circle, its pilot obviously seeking a way down through the murk.

'Target is heading north and climbing, skipper. Range half a mile. Steer three-three-zero.'

The enemy pilot had given up his attempt to land at Spayer and was now flying off in search of an alternative airfield. He kept on varying his height, sometimes dropping down to three thousand feet and then shooting up to six thousand.

'He's an inconsistent bastard, isn't he?' Bowen commented mildly.

'He's dead ahead now,' Wells said. 'Six hundred yards.'

Bowen peered through the windshield into the darkness. 'Can't see the bugger,' he muttered, his voice exasperated.

'Still at six hundred yards, dead ahead.'

Bowen took the Mosquito down a couple of hundred feet. The target was now only three hundred yards away, above and slightly to port. The pilot made a conscious effort to relax, to let his eyes rove across the patch of sky ahead without staring.

Then, suddenly, he had it. It was nothing more than a darker patch against the night sky, but to Bowen's trained eye it was unmistakably an aircraft. He would not lose it now. He opened the throttles slightly to close the range still further, and pressed the R/T button.

'Bogey, bogey, waggle your wings.' He made the call continuously as the distance between the two aircraft decreased. The radio was tuned to a frequency known as Command Guard; in theory, Bowen's call should be picked up by any RAF aircraft within radio range. As an aid to identification, and as an insurance against being shot down by a friendly fighter, they would rock their wings several times.

The wings of the aircraft ahead, now clearly visible, stayed level. Wells, abandoning his radar set for the moment, had seen it too, and was checking off its characteristics out loud.

'Monoplane . . . twin engines . . . single fin and rudder . . .' He exploded in sudden fury. 'Oh, shit, skipper! It's another Mossie!'

Bowen was afraid that his navigator was right, but he wanted to make absolutely certain. The range narrowed to less than one hundred yards, and what he saw tended only to confirm his navigator's suspicions. The target aircraft's engines were set well forward, their spinners protruding some distance ahead of a fairly short nose, just like a Mosquito's.

Brilliant flashes split the darkness, and twin trails of tracer lanced towards him. Frantically, he kicked the rudder and shoved the stick over to one side. The Mossie swerved violently and the glowing tracers streaked past its starboard wingtip.

No Mosquito had rearward-firing guns.

'Okay, skipper, I've still got him. Left, ten degrees off the nose, descending.'

Bowen pulled the Mosquito round and quickly picked up the other aircraft again. It was in a shallow dive, heading for the cloud cover. More tracer spat at him; he ignored it and pressed the gun button as the shadowy target came into his sights. The Mosquito's four cannon opened up with a terrific roar, their recoil pounding up through the cockpit floor and making the crew's feet ache. Bowen kept his thumb on the button and saw his shells strike home, sparkling on the target's dark silhouette.

Flames streamed back from both its engines, lighting up the black cross on the fuselage. Flaming débris whirled back past the Mosquito's cockpit. The enemy aircraft plummeted into the cloud, and a few moments later Bowen and Wells caught sight of a flash below them, bright enough to penetrate the murk.

Bowen glanced at his fuel gauges, and asked Wells to give him a course for home.

'That sod nearly had us fooled, Alan,' he said. 'We'd better make a point of telling the lads to brush up on their aircraft recognition.'

'What was it?' Wells asked.

'Messerschmitt 410. The bastards have two machine-guns in rearward-firing barbettes on the fuselage sides as well as four cannon in the nose. That one might easily have had us nailed, instead of the other way round.'

They landed at Burningham an hour later and, after shedding their flying clothing and making out their combat reports, made straight for the mess bar. It was packed with officers from both squadrons, and a silence fell as they walked in. They stopped, puzzled, and looked around.

'What's going on?' Bowen asked.

George Yeoman came forward from the crowd at the bar, grinning. He had a bottle of whiskey in each hand.

'Congratulations, chaps,' he said. 'We've been saving these for a special occasion, and this is it. As of two hours ago, the Burningham Wing is now officially part of No. 100 Group, and you've just scored our first victory.'

The crowd had formed a tight ring around the two men, and Bowen sensed that some fun and games were in the offing. A spontaneous party was brewing up, and it was just what they all needed, for the disaster of three weeks earlier was still fresh in their minds.

'Freddie,' Yeoman said to the Intelligence Officer, 'a tankard, if you please.' Barnes produced one, and Yeoman filled it with the spirit. He handed it to Bowen.

'But I don't drink whiskey,' Bowen complained. Yeoman grinned at him evilly.

'Oh, you will, dear boy,' he said. 'You will.'

No. 100 Group, RAF, came into being on 8 November 1943. Its motto was 'Confound and Destroy', which admirably summed up its role of bomber support. From now on, every big bombing attack on Germany would be accompanied by four-engined aircraft of 100 Group—Halifaxes, Stirlings or Flying Fortresses, a small number of which had been acquired from the Americans—fitted with electronic jamming equipment designed to sow confusion among the enemy radars.

At the same time, Mosquito night fighters would range far

and wide over occupied Europe, guarding the flanks of the bomber streams and loitering in the vicinity of the radio beacons over which the enemy fighters assembled. Operating singly, they would also strike hard and fast at the Luftwaffe's airfields, howling down out of the darkness like banshees. The attentions of the prowling Mosquitos made enemy night fighter operations a nightmare, for no airfield in Germany or the occupied territories was safe from these sudden lightning attacks.

The only squadron within the expanding framework of No. 100 Group which was not earmarked for night operations was No. 380. Instead, beginning early in November, the squadron—once again up to full strength after the disaster of 14 October—embarked on a series of fast low-level operations, known as Day Rangers, against targets in France and the Low Countries. None of these sorties were flown east of the Rhine, but the targets attacked were often heavily defended and two Mosquitos were lost in the space of a fortnight. The first casualty was Sergeant Keen, who was trapped by Messerschmitt 109s during a sortie along the west bank of the Rhine in search of likely targets and shot down; he and his navigator were both killed. Then, a few days later, Flying Officer Collins, O'Grady's replacement, apparently blew himself up in the explosion of his own bombs during an attack on a radar station at Vannes. The theory was that the bombs' delayed-action fuses had failed to work.

The sortie rate was high, but Yeoman sensed a growing air of discontent among his crews. It was understandable, for they had reached a high level of efficiency in their primary role of bomber support and now they were being frittered away, wastefully it seemed, in pin-prick attacks that could just as easily have been carried out by the tactical Mosquitos of No. 2 Group.

The view was shared by Yeoman himself, although he remained silent and, by his own example, tried to encourage his men to get on with the job without question. Privately, he could not help but question the wisdom of his superiors.

Yeoman, however, was not in possession of all the facts. Had the Squadron been employed in long-range attacks against enemy airfields during this period, its loss rate would undoubtedly have been far higher, and this was something the planners in a certain and very secret section of the Air Ministry wished to avoid. Unknown to Yeoman and his crews, events in the air war over Europe were about to take a dramatic new turn—one which might throw the growing Allied air superiority into serious jeopardy. No. 380 Squadron was, in fact, being held in reserve for a very special operation—one whose outcome might mean the difference between life and death for hundreds of British and American airmen.

'I cannot emphasize too strongly, gentlemen, that what you are about to see has the highest security classification. No word of it must ever be uttered outside this room.'

Yeoman and Rothbury nodded. They were seated in an underground room in Whitehall, faced by a civilian whose name they did not know. Apart from the chairs on which they sat, a film projector and a small screen, the green-walled room was completely barren.

The civilian took position behind the Bell and Howell projector and switched it on, at the same time reaching out with his other hand to turn off the room's solitary electric bulb. The projector began to whirr loudly and the three men fixed their eyes on the screen as the first frames danced over it.

They were looking out over an airfield, along the length of a runway. A sleek, twin-engined aircraft raced towards them and pulled up over the camera, leaving twin trails of black smoke. The camera followed it as it dwindled to a distant speck, then it turned and came for a low run across the field, a streak of fluid movement that set Yeoman's pulses racing with excitement. Beside him, Rothbury gave a startled exclamation, and with good reason.

The mysterious aircraft had no propellers.

It was coming in to land now, and Yeoman saw that it had a nosewheel undercarriage, similar to the American Lockheed Lightning. It touched down effortlessly and the two RAF men got a good look at it as it taxied clear of the runway. The fuselage was long and slender, terminating in a single fin with the tailplane set high upon it. The two engine nacelles were sleek, too, although to the eyes of Yeoman and Rothbury they looked somewhat bizarre because of the total absence of spinners and propeller blades. The machine, which appeared to be a single-seater—Yeoman noted professionally that the cockpit was set well forward on the nose, giving good visibility—was camouflaged and bore RAF markings, with the letter 'P' inside a circle on the rear fuselage.

The brief film came to an end and a series of numbers flashed across the screen. The civilian turned on the light again. He was a relatively young man, dapper and upright, with a crispness of voice that betrayed a military background. He also appeared to know what he was talking about scientifically.

'Well, gentlemen,' he said, 'there you have it. The prototype of Britain's first operational reaction fighter.'

'A jet aircraft,' Yeoman commented, his pulse still racing with the excitement of what he had just seen.

The civilian gave a little smile. 'That's the popular name for the concept,' he said, 'but personally I don't think it will ever catch on. Reaction aircraft sounds so much more proper, don't you think? Anyhow, the aircraft has been designed by Gloster's and represents a considerable advance over any fighter we have in service at the moment. It has been allocated the provisional name of "Meteor".'

'When will it be in squadron service?' The question came from Wing Commander Rothbury.

The civilian frowned. 'Not much before the middle of 1944,' he said, 'and that is assuming that the flight test programme runs to schedule. That's the trouble, you see; although we were the first to develop successful reaction engines, we think that the Germans have stolen a march on us in the development of operational aircraft. Would you be good enough to come with me?'

He led the way into an adjoining room. This one was much better furnished, with the rows of leather seats facing a large built-in screen. There were maps around the walls, some of them covered by drapes. Another projector stood in the middle of the room, just behind the seats. 'Please sit down again, gentlemen,' the civilian instructed them. 'I am going to show you some photographs.'

They took their seats, and the civilian began to run through a series of slides. The first depicted a well-equipped airfield, with a good runway complex, permanent hangars and clusters of adjacent buildings.

'That is Peenemünde, on the Baltic coast,' the civilian explained. 'This reconnaissance photograph was taken last July, and if you examine it closely, concentrating on a point immediately below the large hangar on the extreme right, you will see some very curious aeroplanes indeed.'

The two seated men leaned forward, focusing on the spot indicated by the civilian. It was occupied by a pair of weird-looking machines. They appeared to be virtually all wing, which had swept surfaces, and they were very small. It was not difficult to obtain an idea of their size, for a Junkers 88 bomber parked close by dwarfed them.

'We think that they may be rocket-powered,' the civilian said, 'because the dark streaks you can see on the concrete near them have been interpreted by our experts as scorch marks. As yet, we know nothing about them except their approximate wingspan, which is about thirty feet.

'We had known for a long time that the Germans were developing secret weapons at Peenemünde,' he went on, 'which is why Bomber Command mounted a heavy attack on the place in August. It looks somewhat different now.'

Another slide flicked on the screen, and Yeoman let out a low whistle. The scene was one of total devastation, with the skeletal ruins of buildings standing amid a cratered lunar landscape. The stark black-and-white photograph captured, with awful clarity, the devastating effect of a concentrated attack by seven hundred heavy bombers.

'Now,' the civilian continued, 'take a close look at this one.'

Once again, the next slide depicted two aircraft. Like the previous photographs, this was a vertical shot, taken from many thousands of feet. The enemy machines, their outlines blurred because the picture had been greatly blown up, had swept wings and twin engines.

'This was taken over the Messerschmitt test field at Rechlin four days ago,' the civilian said. 'The aircraft are powered by reaction engines and, as you will note from the shadows under them, appear to have tricycle undercarriages. They are similar in size to the Gloster aircraft you saw a few minutes ago and may well be the type our intelligence sources have listed under the designation Messerschmitt 262, although we are not certain about that.

'This, however, is the photograph that immediately concerns us.'

Again it was a shot of an airfield, taken from high altitude. It showed several aircraft, identifiable as Junkers 88s, Heinkel IIIs and a couple of Junkers 52 transports—and four of the bat-winged aircraft previously photographed at Peenemünde.

'The airfield you see here is Bad Zwischenahn, near Oldenburg. It is very heavily defended, and the pilot who secured these photographs very narrowly escaped with his life. But let him tell you the story himself.'

He pressed a buzzer, and a few moments later a door opened, admitting another civilian followed by a tall, ginger-haired flying officer. The latter appeared slightly nervous, as though he didn't know what this was all about, but then he relaxed, lit up a cigarette given to him by Rothbury, and told what he knew. He was one of that small band of intrepid men who, flying stripped-down Spitfires and Mosquitos, roved across Europe and deep into Germany, their cameras uncovering the enemy's secrets. Operating at altitudes of up to 40,000 feet, they had little to fear from enemy fighters. If one was sighted, the reconnaissance pilot usually had only to open his throttle and climb away out of range. That was the recipe for survival, for the reconnaissance aircraft carried no defensive armament.

'It was two days ago,' the ginger-haired pilot said. 'November the twentieth. I was briefed to fly a circular route over western Germany, photographing three airfields: Rheine, Ahlhorn and Zwishenahn. It was a fairly routine show until I got over the last one.

'I'd just completed my photo run when I saw a thick contrail, about a mile away horizontally and maybe seven or eight thousand feet lower down. It curved towards me and then disappeared, so I opened the taps and climbed as hard as I could. Three minutes later I was up to 42,000 feet. When I looked back, I saw that the other aircraft was closing fast. I don't mind telling you, it nearly gave me heart failure.

'I could see it clearly now, and it was the funniest-looking damn thing I've ever come across. It was all wing, and looked just like one of those paper aeroplanes we used to make when we were kids.

'It came straight towards me, going like a bat out of hell. Christ, it must have been doing 600 mph! It opened fire, and I did the only thing possible under the circumstances—I started turning like hell, knowing that nothing could out-turn a Spit at this altitude.

'Anyhow, he missed, thank God, and shot underneath me. I lost sight of him a minute later; he was heading back towards the deck, pretty fast.'

The reconnaissance pilot's brow furrowed. 'Funny thing, though,' he said thoughtfully. 'It wasn't leaving a contrail any more. Can't understand that. It frightened me fartless, though. If that thing had been scrambled to intercept me, it must have climbed to 40,000 feet in five minutes flat. But that's impossible, isn't it?' He looked questioningly at Rothbury and Yeoman, as though searching for some reassurance.

'Thank you, Flying Officer,' the civilian said. 'We'll be in touch with you again, if we need any further information from you.' He opened the door and the ginger-haired pilot left, looking more perplexed than ever.

After the pilot had gone, the civilian said to Yeoman and Rothbury: 'There you have it, gentlemen. That's all we know; the rest is conjecture. What we believe, however, is that these aircraft are the prototypes of a radical new interceptor, and the reconnaissance pilot's account tends to substantiate the theory that it is rocket-powered and very, very fast. We think that the story of the enemy aircraft's vapour trail suddenly disappearing is significant; if it is indeed rocket-powered, its motor is likely to have enough fuel for only a few minutes under full power—in other words, enough time for it to climb to altitude. After that, it is probably designed to make its attack in a fast glide. If the reconnaissance pilot's estimate of a speed of 600 mph is accurate, you may imagine what a threat several squadrons of these machines would pose to the Allied bombing offensive, and to the American daylight bombers in particular.'

He paused, toying with a pen for a few moments. Then he continued:

'As I said earlier, this is only conjecture—but we think that the Germans have set up an experimental unit at Zwischenahn to test these new aircraft in action. The reconnaissance photographs revealed four of them; there may be more. Because of its revolutionary nature, however, it is unlikely that the enemy will order the new machine into mass production until it has been proven under operational conditions.'

He looked meaningfully at the two pilots. 'If those prototypes can be destroyed,' he said slowly, 'it could buy time for us. Several months of time—enough to enable us to build some form of effective countermeasures against them.

'Before long,' the civilian went on, 'the Americans will have brought into service several squadrons of a new long-range escort fighter, the P-51 Mustang. The type has already been operational for some time, but as a ground-attack and reconnaissance machine. The new escort version, however, will be able to accompany the daylight bomber formations as far as Berlin and back; it will also be able to keep the Luftwaffe's fighter airfields in a constant state of harassment by day, complementing the RAF's long-range intruder effort by night. If the enemy brings his new fighter types into large-scale service, our only chance will be to keep them pinned on the ground, to seek them out and destroy them wherever they can be found, for we will have little hope of meeting them on equal terms in the air until aircraft such as the Meteor become available.'

The civilian looked hard at Yeoman. 'Do you think, Squadron Leader, that your squadron will be capable of carrying out an attack on Zwischenahn—an attack in broad daylight, to ensure the destruction of the new prototypes?'

Yeoman removed his unlit pipe from his mouth and gave a non-committal grunt. 'That's hard to say,' he commented, bringing a rather disapproving sideways look from Rothbury. 'What I mean to say is, we can knock out these new Hun aircraft all right, so long as we know where to look for them—and provided we can get through to them. It will take some planning, and we'd need some back-up: diversionary attacks, and all that sort of thing. The weather might be in our favour, though; plenty of cloud cover at this time of year.'

He tapped the stem of his pipe thoughtfully against his teeth, his keen and experienced mind already turning over the beginnings of several attack plans. Fighters might not present too much of a problem, especially if the Mosquitos could retain a fair element of surprise and a diversion could be laid on. Flak would be the main worry; if Zwischenahn was important to the enemy, the place would be stiff with it.

His fears were confirmed that afternoon, during a fuller briefing held elsewhere in the building. This was a purely RAF affair, presided over by Group Captain Sampson. Together, they pored over all available reconnaissance photographs of Zwischenahn, taken during the past weeks. The enemy gun positions were indicated by arrows, and there were a lot of them. Yeoman also noted that the Germans had set up flak lanes, extending for as much as two miles outwards from the ends of the runways, so that anything attempting to shoot up a German aircraft as it approached to land would have to negotiate a savage curtain of anti-aircraft fire.

Apart from the rocket fighters, several other Luftwaffe units were based on Zwischenahn. There was a transport squadron, and what appeared to be a communications flight, but Yeoman was not interested in them. What captured his attention, and increased his grim determination to make a success of this mission, was the information that two squadrons of fighters—one of Focke-Wulf 190s and the other of Messerschmitt 109Gs—had recently been moved to Zwischenahn from Holland, presumably to undertake the primary role of airfield defence.

They had been identified as belonging to Fighter Wing 301.

Chapter Ten

JOACHIM RICHTER WAS FEELING FAR FROM CONFIDENT. HIS breakfast felt like lead in his stomach, he had slept badly and he was surrounded by an aura of impending disaster which he found quite impossible to shake off.

He had been attached to Special Commando 16 for a month now, and it was entirely his own fault. At the beginning of November, quite out of the blue, he had been summoned to the Reich Air Ministry in Berlin, where a lieutenant-general had asked him if he would like to volunteer for special duties. He would not have to relinquish his command of Fighter Wing 301, but simply be detached from it for a while.

The general explained that experienced fighter pilots were being brought in from all over the Luftwaffe and given the opportunity to participate in what he called an Advanced Fighter Course. It would, he said, involve one of Germany's new secret weapons—one which, if successful, would smash the American bomber formations from the sky. So Richter had agreed, and now he was wishing that he had not.

For a start, he had been virtually sent back to school, spending nearly three weeks in the classroom while a mixture of Luftwaffe specialists and scientists explained the peculiarities of the Messerschmitt Me 163A rocket fighter in minute detail. They had sounded convincing enough, but Richter had soon come to realize that the 163 had an awful lot of peculiarities, quite apart from its radical appearance. Its handling characteristics were different from those of an orthodox aircraft and it sat on a trolley-type undercarriage which was jettisoned after take-off, the landing being made on a retractable skid. One had to get the landing right first time, too, for the technique was to glide in once the rocket fuel had been exhausted.

Then there was the rocket motor itself, and the fuel that powered it. The Me 163's tanks were filled with hydrogen peroxide and water and a catalyst, hydrazine hydrate and methyl alcohol, a lethal combination which, when blended, exploded in the rocket's combustion chamber to produce several thousand pounds of thrust. If anything went wrong, however... one of the instructors had made the point better than any words by pouring a thimbleful of one fuel into a similar quantity of the other. There had been a loud bang and a searing flame had shot right across the room.

Their heads spinning with mathematical formulae, the volunteers had then made several flights in a glider version of the Me 163, called the Hawk. They had been towed into the air behind a Messerschmitt 110 and then released, gliding down to land. Each volunteer had also learned how to work the controls of the rocket motor on a special static rig, and then had come the big day when they were to start their powered flying.

One of the instructors had gone up first, just to show them how it should be done. They had watched carefully as his aircraft was fuelled, had seen him climb into the tiny cockpit with its screwed-down canopy. Dragging a long streamer of flame, the 163 had shrieked down the runway and pulled up in a dizzying climb, dwindling with incredible speed at the tip of an arrow-straight smoke trail.

The trail had ended abruptly, at a height of seven thousand feet, in a black bubble that burst across the sky. The sound of the explosion reached the watchers a few seconds later.

Another instructor had made a successful flight, however, and so had the first of the volunteers. Now, the next morning, it was Richter's turn.

Johnny Schumacher, now a captain and in command of JG 301's No. 1 Squadron, had come over from the other side of the airfield to watch the fun. He was cheerfully cynical about Richter's chances of survival.

'School for Advanced Suicide,' he remarked, as he watched Richter struggle into the specially-impregnated PC flying overall, designed to protect him if he was splashed accidentally by any of the rocket fuel.

'Can I have your collection of pipes, if you don't come back?'

Richter glared at him, although his friend's presence had the effect of steadying his nerves. 'No, you can't,' he grunted. 'They're for big men to smoke, not little boys.'

An instructor poked his head round the door of the crew room, indicating that it was time to go. Richter nodded at Schumacher, grinning, and walked outside.

'Break your neck and legs,' Schumacher called after him, wishing him good fortune in the traditional Luftwaffe manner.

Richter and the instructor walked out to the waiting Me 163. It looked deceptively innocent as it stood at the end of the runway, painted the colour of the pale blue December sky, with darker patches of grey on the upper surfaces of its wings and fuselage. On its nose, within a white shield, was painted a man in red hunting jacket and black riding boots, seated astride a flaming cannonball: the legendary Baron Munchausen, whose fictitious ride through the sky had become the well-chosen symbol of Special Commando 16.

Richter climbed into the cockpit, did up his harness and intercom leads and switched on the electrics. Standing on the wing, his instructor bent over him with a few final words of advice.

'Remember, Herr Major, keep the stick in the neutral position during the take-off. There is no need for any movement; the aircraft will fly itself off the ground. Drop your wheels at ten metres, no lower, or they might bounce up again and hit you. Wait until the speed reaches 800 km/h, then pull back steadily on the stick. Remember to report as you pass each thousand metres. Hold the climb until the motor cuts, then level out.'

139

He tapped Richter encouragingly on the shoulder. 'Right, that's all. You're on your own.'

The broad cockpit canopy slammed down into position over him and he locked it into place. He made sure that his oxygen mask was firmly fixed over his face, checked the instruments and then signalled to the mechanics who were standing by the accumulator. A moment later, there was a low whistle as the fuel pump turbine began to revolve; it swelled to a whine and then to a piercing howl. Richter gave another signal and the mechanics unplugged the accumulator, hastily moving back to a safe distance.

Taking a deep breath, Richter opened the throttle, allowing the two volatile rocket fuels to mix. There was a thump as the first of the rocket chambers ignited, a two-second delay that seemed like an eternity, and then, as Richter threw a pair of switches, the motor blasted into full roaring life.

With a will of its own the Me 163 hurtled down the runway with an acceleration that pressed him back into his seat. He had the weirdest feeling of being nothing more than a spectator, with no control over his destiny or that of the speeding machine. He needed to make no control movements at all; the 163 sped along the blurring tarmac like a bullet.

At nearly 300 km/h it left the ground. Richter forced himself to wait for a moment, then threw the switch that jettisoned the undercarriage. There was the briefest of jolts, and now the needle of the air speed indicator wound round the dial with phenomenal speed. The ground was a green streak, flowing past him, barely glimpsed at the periphery of his vision.

The ASI needle approached 800 km/h and he eased back the stick, ever so gently. The 163's nose came up and suddenly he was lying almost on his back as the little aircraft raced into the blue vault of the sky on its long pillar of smoke. The thunder of its engine came to him only as a faint rumble, but he knew that in the little lakeside town of Bad Zwischenahn its fearsome crescendo would be rattling the rooftops.

Two thousand metres already! Remembering his instructions, he hastily pressed the R/T button.

'Bat to Tulip. Rak-wagons Two.'

The controller at Zwischenahn acknowledged curtly. Richter, his earlier fears forgotten, was seized by a sudden wild exhilaration as the 163 continued straight up in that seemingly endless climb, with the whole of space ahead of it. They called the little aircraft the Komet, and how apt it was! What would old Munchausen have made of this!

'Rak-wagons six . . . Rak-wagons eight . . .' The thousands of metres unrolled in his wake. He was master of the world, of the sky. 'Rak-wagons nine . . . Rak-wagons ten . . . eleven . . .'

At 36,500 feet, 11,000 metres, the rocket motor finally cut out, its fuel exhausted. The acceleration dropped away sharply and the seat harness began to tug at Richter as gravity reasserted itself. He pulled the throttle back and levelled out, calling up control to report his peak altitude, then decided to spend a few minutes trying out the 163's controls.

The little rocket plane handled beautifully. He eased the stick right back to induce a stall, but there was no abrupt nose-down pitch; instead, the Komet remained in a level attitude, losing height.

He was still above 9,000 metres, so he pushed forward the stick to investigate the 163's behaviour in a dive. The speed built up again rapidly until the ASI showed nearly 1,000 km/h and the needle of the adjacent Machmeter, measuring the aircraft's speed in relation to the speed of sound, showed .83.

As he levelled out, he realized with a profound shock that he had just joined a small and select band of pilots who were the fastest men in the world. He had reached a speed that was a good one-third higher than that of the fastest piston-engined fighter.

He zoomed up and dived again, the speed falling away slowly as he brought the Komet down towards Zwischenahn, trying out various manœuvres. There were no snags, no control problems at all.

Visibility was good, and he had no trouble in picking out the glittering lake beside which the town and its nearby airfield nestled. In a steady glide now, he brought the Komet down to fifteen hundred metres and lined up with the runway.

There was no need for any turns to shed excess height; the approach was perfect. He pointed the nose at the big white cross on the runway that indicated his touch-down point, holding the Komet steady as it dropped through the last five hundred metres, lowering the skid and the flaps as he came up to the airfield boundary.

He misjudged the last phase of the landing slightly, but it didn't matter.

He raised the nose very slightly as the white cross flashed underneath him, and an instant later there was a slight crunch as the Komet's skid made contact with the runway. He held the wings level as the aircraft skidded along the surface for several hundred metres and then, as it slid to a stop, he allowed the port wingtip to settle gently on the ground.

The ground crew support vehicle drew up alongside, pulling the trailer on which the Komet would be removed, and the mechanics helped Richter from the cockpit. His instructor, a Messerschmitt test pilot attached to the Luftwaffe, came up to him and smiled broadly.

'Well, Herr Major, what did you think of it?'

Richter's enthusiasm was boundless. 'Fantastic! I can't begin to describe it—the speed, the sheer exhilaration!'

His brain was working overtime. 'Just imagine what we could do with a few hundred of these machines, a thousand even, all armed with a battery of air-to-air rockets and cannon... why, we'd rip the Amis to shreds. Nothing they have could touch us!'

He became suddenly serious and gripped the other man's arm. They stopped in their tracks and looked at one another.

'But it has to be now, Dorner. There's no time to be lost.' He lowered his voice, glancing around rapidly to make sure that no one else could hear. He had known the test pilot for some time, and the two men were in agreement on many matters, some of which were best left unspoken.

'You know as well as I do, Dorner, that things are not going well for us. Italy is out of the war, and we are having to divert more and more divisions to hold the Allies there; disaster after disaster confronts us in Russia; and it can only be a question of time before the British and Americans attempt an invasion on the Western Front. Two years ago, we believed that Japan's offensives in the Pacific would keep the Americans occupied while we dealt with the British and the Russians, but now it is the Japanese who are being defeated.'

The other nodded slowly. 'We cannot fight the whole world,' he said, 'and hope to win. The best we can hope for now is to force the Allies into an armistice. . . . There is talk of a new secret weapon, something so devastating that it could end the war overnight. Perhaps if—'

Richter cut him short with the wave of a hand. 'I don't believe in things I can't see,' he said contemptuously. 'Now this'—he indicated the Me 163—'this is different. Here we have a weapon which will make the Allies think twice. Just think, Dorner! With a thousand of these, and a thousand of the new Me 262 jet fighters, we could sweep the Allies from our skies in six months! Our war industries could function again without interruption . . . there would no longer be any fear of an Allied invasion in the west, and we could devote all our attentions to smashing the Soviets.'

His face became grim, and a shadow passed over his eyes. 'There is our real enemy, Dorner. Soviet Russia. In that, I agree implicitly with the Führer. I have served there, and I know. The sights I have seen . . .'

He came back to the present with a visible effort. 'Time, Dorner. Time is running out for the Fatherland. So we must buy some more, with aircraft such as these.'

He looked back once more at the little rocket fighter, then up at the sky. Softly, he said: 'We are here to prove ourselves, Dorner, and we must do it quickly. We must have these weapons in sufficient numbers before the summer of next year; that will be the critical time. Otherwise it will be too late. For all of us.'

Chapter Eleven

IT WAS FIVE DAYS TO CHRISTMAS; THE FIFTH CHRISTMAS OF
the war. For nearly two weeks snow and sleet had fallen in
an almost continuous blanket over north-west Europe, bringing air operations to a standstill, but now, on 20 December,
the leaden clouds had lifted and watery shafts of sunlight
poked through occasional rifts in the overcast. Runways were
cleared, crews once again crowded the briefing-rooms, and
the war-song of powerful engines resounded in the wintry
sky.

The Mosquitos flew midway between sea and cloud, cleav-
ing their way through the icy air, little rainbows of moisture
dancing on the glittering tips of their propellers. There were
sixteen of them, for a new flight of four aircraft had been
added to the strength of No. 380 Squadron, such was the
importance attached to this mission.

The new flight, bringing up the rear of the formation, was
led by Wing Commander Rothbury; the other pilots were
Flying Officers Pearce and Tilson and Sergeant Van Kleve,
the latter a Belgian.

Apart from them, the formation consisted, more or less,
of the old team. Yeoman, Miller, Saint and Laurie, leading
in Red Section; Sloane and Lorrimer in Blue Section, together

with two new pilots named Hudson and Carr, who had replaced Collins and Keen; and Yellow Section, with Mc-Manners, Reed, Romilly and Olafsson.

Looking out of the cockpit beyond the thumping windscreen wipers—it was necessary to keep them working, otherwise an opaque layer of ice crystals destroyed visibility—Yeoman scanned the murky horizon and felt anxiety building up inside him. The Met. people had predicted that an unbroken layer of cloud would extend all the way over the North Sea and deep into Germany, reaching from 1,500 to 8,500 feet above sea-level, but it was not working out like that at all. Ahead, over the North German coast, the clouds were already beginning to disperse, and a band of yellow light spread slowly over the sea as the sun struggled through.

The attack plan called for the Mosquitos to penetrate enemy territory near the island of Norderney, skirting Wittmundhaven airfield and covering the forty miles to Zwischenahn at low level. Oblique photographs, brought back by a Spitfire of the Photographic Reconnaissance Unit the previous day—its pilot dropping down from the clouds to make a single run before climbing into their shelter once more—had revealed that the enemy rocket planes were concentrated in a single hangar on the south-east edge of the airfield; open doors had obligingly yielded a glimpse of them. This hangar was to be attacked by the four Mosquitos of Yeoman's section, while other airfield installations—particularly the hangars thought to contain the fighters of JG 301—were to be hit by Blue and Yellow Sections. Wing Commander Rothbury's Green Section, attacking last of all, would go for the fuel dump and plug any gaps left by the first three sections.

After the attack, the retreating Mosquitos—heading straight out across Holland—were originally to have been covered by four squadrons of American Thunderbolt fighters, but this supporting force had been called off at the last moment because of the weather conditions, the idea being that the Mosquitos would have the benefit of plenty of cloud cover.

All that was now changed; the weather forecast was proving completely wrong. The Mosquitos would have to fight their way out alone. But there was no time to worry about that now.

Ten miles from Norderney, Yeoman knew with grim certainty that the element of surprise was lost. A German minesweeper, probably sweeping the approaches to the Ems River, threw some shells at them as they streaked past, skimming the sea; the shells were wide of the mark, but there was no doubt that the enemy vessel would be signalling their presence to bases on shore.

Flak rose to meet them in evil, twisting ropes of smoke as they sped over the coast, and claimed its first victim three miles north-east of Emden. A shell burst in front of the nose of Pilot Officer Reed's Mosquito, flying number two to McManners in Yellow Section, and for a few moments it seemed that no damage had been done, for there was no smoke or fire and the aircraft continued to hold its station. Then, with awful finality, it turned over on its back and dived inverted into the bank of a river, vanishing in the explosion of its bombs.

Yves Romilly, in number three position, glanced back briefly at the funeral pyre. Then, his eyes expressionless above his oxygen mask, he closed in beside the leader's aircraft.

It was Van Kleve, in Rothbury's Green Section, who broke radio silence.

'Fighters astern, seven o'clock!'

There were half a dozen of them, Focke-Wulf 190s, curving down out of a sky that was now almost completely blue, diving at high speed to overhaul the Mosquitos. Already, they were dangerously close.

In a fraction of a second, Rothbury made his decision. Telling Pearce to take over command of the section, he pushed the throttle levers through the gate to full combat boost and stood the Mosquito on its wingtip, pulling round steeply to meet the attackers. In the seconds before they were on him he opened the bomb doors, jettisoned his pair of 500-pounders, then snapped the doors shut again and headed straight for the leading Focke-Wulf, firing with cannon and machine-guns. The enemy pilot, taken by surprise, pulled up sharply and took the full burst of high explosive in his belly, splitting open like a ripe tomato. His wings folded and he plunged into the ground in a blossom of flame, crimson against the snow.

Rothbury was attacked simultaneously by two more Focke-Wulfs and he turned towards them, firing as one flicked across his sights. He thought he saw fragments break from it, and then the fighter whirled away out of sight.

The Mosquito shuddered as shells slammed into it. It was being attacked from all sides as the remaining enemy pilots came at it vengefully, the other Mosquitos temporarily ignored. The battle was so low now that the wingtips of the whirling machines were almost brushing the treetops, and Rothbury knew that he could not possibly survive for much longer.

The Mosquito's port engine cowling flew off with a terrific bang and blinding flames streamed back. The pilot ruddered frantically, levelling the aircraft, barely able to control it. A small copse rushed to meet him and the Mosquito's belly crunched through the tops of some pine trees. Rothbury closed both the throttles and, as the last vestige of control disappeared, covered his face with both arms.

The impact was suprisingly gentle. The Mosquito ploughed across a field, throwing up a great wake of snow, and embedded its nose in a drift.

Pulling his dazed senses together, Rothbury reached up and pulled a red lever in front of the roof panel, then undid his straps and pushed at the square of perspex with all his strength. It fell away to one side and snow trickled into the cockpit.

German snow, thought Rothbury, and followed his navigator up through the hatch, slithering on to the partly-covered wing. Smoke from the burning port engine drifted over them.

It was bitterly cold. There was a sudden fierce barking and a huge Alsatian came bounding through the drifts. Thirty yards behind it was a man, carrying a rifle. He stopped and raised the weapon to his shoulder.

Wearily, Rothbury and his navigator put up their hands.

The remaining Mosquitos thundered on, the roar of their engines dislodging snow in miniature avalanches from the roofs of the hamlets over which they passed. The surviving Focke-Wulfs had once more taken up the chase, but now they were well astern; Rothbury's desperate sacrifice had bought thirty seconds of time, and it was enough. On the horizon, a small black patch against the white background, was Zwischenahn Lake. The enemy fighters would not catch the Mosquitos before they reached their target.

Joachim Richter was in Zwischenahn's control tower, checking on the latest weather situation, when the red telephone that connected the field to Divisional Operations HQ shrilled. A lieutenant answered it, and immediately hit the button that set the alarm klaxons blaring all over the airfield. To Richter, he shouted: 'Mosquitos! Heading this way!'

Not waiting to hear any more, Richter threw himself down the stairs and into a waiting staff car, telling the driver to step on the gas.

'Where to, Herr Major?' the man queried, as the car skidded away towards the hangars on the other side of the airfield.

'To the nearest fighter!' Richter yelled. 'Focke-Wulf or Messerschmitt, it makes no difference!'

He cursed fluently. If only one of the Me 163s had been fuelled and ready to go! But the rocket fighters had not flown for several days, because of the bad weather.

Two flights of Focke-Wulfs, which were always held at readiness, were already beginning to taxi round the perimeter track to the end of the runway. Normally, in an urgent situation like this, they would have taken off straight from their dispersal area across the grass, but because of the snow this was not possible.

They were still taxi-ing when the first Mosquitos arrived overhead in a thunderclap of sound, their coming heralded by a mighty anti-aircraft barrage that covered the northern sky in black cauliflower clusters of shellbursts. The attackers sped on, skimming the airfield boundary, boxed in by the angry constellations of twinkling flashes, blossoming smoke and the glowing lines of tracer, and it seemed impossible that they could survive, yet survive they did.

Yeoman fought to hold his aircraft steady as it rode the concussions, his thumb pressed on the gun button, using the fountains of snow kicked up by his shells and bullets to help him gauge the distance to his target—the low camouflaged hangar that sheltered the rocket fighters. The Mosquito's bomb doors gaped wide, and the pilot's gloved finger hovered over the bomb release. The hangar swept towards him, and his fingertip moved down sharply. At that precise moment, a giant hammer struck the Mosquito, hurling it brutally to one side. There was a stunning, fearsome crash and the sound of splinters, rattling on wings and fuselage in a deadly drum-roll. Instinctively, Yeoman pulled back the stick, knowing that the bombs must have missed their target.

Behind him, the second shell in the salvo that had almost brought Yeoman to grief exploded squarely under the nose of Flight Sergeant Miller's aircraft. The Mosquito bucked, and Miller felt a terrific blow in his stomach. Blood spurted over the instrument panel, but in the last seconds of his life Miller did not comprehend that it was his own.

His last conscious act was to push the stick forward again, sending the crippled Mosquito hurtling towards the hangar; his last conscious thought being one of regret that he could no longer speak, could not tell Sillitoe that he was sorry.

Shedding a trail of wreckage, the Mosquito plunged through the hangar doors and exploded in the middle of the floor. Streams of burning petrol splashed out to engulf the Me 163s. A split second later the Mosquitos flown by Saint and Laurie howled overhead, their delayed-action bombs plummeting into the middle of the inferno with deadly accuracy.

All six bombs erupted almost simultaneously. The hangar swelled like a balloon and then collapsed in on itself in a pile of tangled metal, crushing everything and everyone inside. A huge column of smoke billowed up, shot with tongues of flame.

The Mosquitos of Blue and Yellow Sections, meanwhile,

arrived over the airfield just as the first Focke-Wulfs were taking off. Ignoring the enemy fighters—there was little that could be done about them without deviating from the attack plan, in any case—the pilots headed straight for the hangars, cannon and machine-guns blazing, spreading out as they came so that their bombs would achieve a wide arc of destruction.

A line of 20-mm shells from one of the hurtling Mosquitos tracked across the airfield and the pilot, Romilly, his lips stretched tight in a mirthless grin, gave a touch of rudder so that his cone of fire reached out towards a staff car, speeding round the perimeter track. Geysers of snow burst upwards, obscuring the vehicle, and when he saw it next it was lying on its side.

The shells, in fact, had not hit the car; the damage had been caused by Richter's driver, who had skidded and over-turned in his frantic efforts to get out of the line of fire. Both men were flung out, but the snow heaped by the side of the perimeter track cushioned their fall and they picked them-selves up, unhurt apart from a few bruises. Crouched in the shelter of their vehicle, they had a grandstand view as the Mosquitos systematically destroyed the airfield. Explosion after explosion crashed out from the wrecked hangars, each sending a fresh column of smoke spurting into the sky to join the black pall that was already covering the field.

Overwhelmed by the disaster, Richter stared dumbly at the heap of crushed and flame-seared metal that had been the hangar housing the Me 163s. The precious prototypes would never fly in combat now, and it would be weeks before others could be made ready.

All the Mosquitos of Blue and Yellow sections miracu-lously came through the storm of flak without serious damage and curved away to the west, jinking as the red, green and yellow lines of glowing shells pursued them across the snow-covered ground.

The three surviving aircraft of Green Section, however, were not so lucky. Bringing up the rear, and trailing some distance behind the rest, they were just coming up to the airfield perimeter when the first of the pursuing Focke-Wulfs, its engine at full boost, caught up with them. The enemy fighter opened fire, a straightforward no-deflection shot, as Flying Officer Tilson's Mosquito came within range. Its shells punched into the port engine, which immediately began to stream white smoke, and ended up in the cockpit.

The Mosquito reared up suddenly, went over on its back and almost completed a loop before it struck the ground with a vivid flash.

The Focke-Wulf, joined now by two or three others which had managed to get off the ground, closed on the other two Mosquitos like angry wasps. Pearce's aircraft took two 20-mm shells in its starboard wing, shattering part of the aileron and causing the flaps to break away. Using all his strength, the pilot managed to retain control and release his bombs over the fuel dump; then, with the aircraft threatening to wind itself into the ground at any moment, he flopped it down on tis belly a few hundred yards further on. As he did so, the rocket fuel tanks in the dump exploded with a brilliant white glare and an explosion that could be heard for miles. A great pillar of white flame shot a thousand feet into the air.

Van Kleve, who bombed the dump a few seconds after Pearce, saw the latter's Mosquito flop into the snow. Snatching a glance back over his shoulder, he saw pilot and navigator struggling clear; then he was away, speeding low over the far boundary of the field.

The Focke-Wulfs pursued him relentlessly and his Mosquito was hit time after time. He went up to three thousand feet, intending to turn and fight, but suddenly the controls went slack in his hands as a burst of cannon fire slammed into the rear fuselage, severing the control cables. He yelled 'Get out!' to his navigator, who punched open the roof hatch and clawed his way through it, his face white with fear.

Van Kleve tried to follow him, but the Mosquito was now spinning wildly and the 'g' forces held the Belgian glued to his seat. Praying hard, he managed to grab both sides of the escape hatch and then, with his feet planted on the instrument panel, he made a last supreme effort and levered his head and shoulders out into the icy air. The slipstream plucked at him and buffeted him, tearing away his senses. Half in and half out of the hatch, gripped relentlessly by the forces that had seized the plunging aircraft, he closed his eyes and waited for the end.

When he opened them again, he was lying in a deep snow-drift, his half-deployed parachute spread around him. The telescoped wreckage of the Mosquito lay fifty yards away, smouldering.

Wincing with the ache of bruised limbs, Van Kleve struggled to his knees. Pulling off his flying helmet, he knelt bareheaded in the snow and gave thanks for his deliverance.

Meanwhile, the ten surviving Mosquitos of Red, Blue and Yellow Sections were well on their way towards the Dutch border, thirty miles from Zwischenahn, the aircraft sliding into their well-rehearsed combat formation as they joined up with the leader. There was about four-tenths cloud over Holland at 15,000 feet and Yeoman took the formation in a fast climb towards it, knowing that it could save their lives if they were attacked. And Yeoman knew for certain that they would be attacked, for their homeward flight would take them close to several enemy fighter airfields—including the three they had hit on the squadron's first daylight operation, four months earlier.

Fifteen miles into Holland, near the village of Berger, they lost another aircraft. The voice of the Terry Saint, flying number two to Yeoman now that Miller had gone, suddenly came up over the R/T.

'We're in trouble. Oil temperature's going off the clock on both engines. Must have caught some flak.'

Yeoman looked round and saw Saint's Mosquito dropping away out of formation. Even as he watched, its starboard propeller windmilled to a stop, and there was an intermittent trail of smoke from the other motor.

'We've had it. Both engines gone. Baling out now.'

'Okay, Terry. Good luck.'

There was nothing else to say. Half a minute later, Olafsson, bringing up the rear of the formation, reported that he had seen two parachutes, far below. Yeoman sighed with relief; it was good to know that the happy-go-lucky New Zealander and his navigator were safe, even if a POW cage lay at the end of their road.

The enemy fighters hit them a few minutes later, coming at them from ahead, slanting down hard and fast to cut off their escape route. Yeoman, seeing at once that there was no possiblity of making a run for it or of reaching cloud cover before they were attacked, ordered the Mosquitos to form a defensive circle, each aircraft covering the tail of the one ahead.

Below, in the streets and fields, people stopped work to watch the desperate merry-go-round that developed high over their heads, heard the chatter of cannon and machine-guns. They saw a Mosquito drop out of the circle, flame pouring from its wings, and disintegrate into spiralling fragments. A moment later it was followed by a Messerschmitt, a dense streamer of white smoke marking its fall.

Yeoman had seen Olafsson die, his aircraft pulverized by the merciless assaults of two Messerschmitts, and almost instantly his own shells had torn a wing off one of the enemy fighters. Then he glanced at the western sky, and his heart sank. Coming at them, in three compact formations, were at least fifty more fighters.

'Now we're for it, Happy,' he said quietly. He knew that he was almost out of ammunition, and he knew that the other Mosquitos must be in a similar plight.

The navigator made no reply. He was leaning forward in his straps, peering intently at the fighters which were pouring down on them like an avalanche. Suddenly, he gave a yell that almost split the pilot's eardrums.

'Thunderbolts! Jesus, skipper, they're Thunderbolts!'

Wild elation surged up inside Yeoman as he saw that Hardy was right. The tubby, radial-engined American fighters fell on the Germans like a pack of wolves, and within a minute savage battles were flaring up all over the sky.

Yeoman looked at Hardy, grinning and wiping the sweat from his face. Then he pressed the R/T button and called up what was left of the squadron.

'All right, chaps, that's it. Let's go home.'

He looked around, identifying the battle-scarred Mosquitos by their code letters.

McManners and Romilly; Laurie, tucked in close to his own wingtip; Sloane, Lorrimer, Hudson and Carr. Was that really all that was left?

Together, they headed out towards the sanctuary of the open sea.

THE END

Epilogue

THE TWO MEN STOOD ON THE VIBRATING DECK OF THE DE-stroyer, watching the sun-drenched rock of Gibraltar receding astern. Ahead of them lay the broad reaches of the Atlantic; behind them, four months of danger and hardship.

The long winter was over, and the spring of 1944 now spread its gentle balm over war-torn Europe. The two men stared at the wake of the destroyer, hardly daring to believe that their ordeal was over; that the weeks of hiding in fear, from Holland to southern France, were little more than a bad memory.

They owed their liberty to so many ordinary people. The steelworker in Amsterdam; the guides who had led them over the border into Belgium; the housewife in Brussels, who had sheltered them in her attic while the tread of the German patrols echoed in the cobbled streets outside.

And there was the woman who had shepherded them through the long, arduous journey across France, from village to village and house to house. A beautiful woman with red hair and wistful green eyes who, amazingly, spoke perfect English with an American accent and whose name was Madeleine.

Terry Saint and his navigator were going home.

THE SERGEANT I:

His assignment was to stop the personnel and supply trains Gen. Erwin Rommel had lined up to checkmate the assault he knew would come on Omaha Beach. His name was the Sergeant—C. J. Mahoney (Code name: Parrot) a big, brawling career GI, an almost perfect killing machine. His first try failed and now he was on a do or die last chance with an explosive loaded train and heading for a fateful rendezvous in a tunnel of death.

Death Train

0   552   11863X   95p

THE SERGEANT 2:

Cherbourg Harbour was the key to the success of the D-Day offensive. If the Allied Forces were denied it as a port of entry for vital armaments and supplies, their campaign would be strangled to death—by Starvation or Wehrmacht counterattack. They dragged "the Sergeant", fresh from the hospital, back to the battlefront to save the harbour.

Hell Harbour

0   552   118648   95p

THE SERGEANT 3:

Maverick "troublemaker" Sgt. C. J. Mahoney and his kill-crazy sidekick, Cranepool, seem to draw all the assignments nobody else can handle. This time, they're sent to bail out Charlie Company of the First Battalion, Fifteenth infantry regiment, which is about to be torn into pieces by the deadly panzer units in Normandy's savage Battle of the Hedgerows.

Bloody Bush

0   052   118656   95p

REIGN OF HELL
by Sven Hassel

Burning, looting, raping, murdering, Hitler's Penal Regiments advanced on the centre of Warsaw leaving in their wake a bloody trail of death and destruction. They killed indiscriminately. Pole or German; young or old; man, woman and child—anyone who crossed their path was eliminated. For Himmler had sworn that Warsaw would be razed to the ground—of it took every member of the German army to do it! And against the Fuhrer's expandable battalions, for whom life had no meaning, the battle for Warsaw became an inferno—an endless reign of terror. . . .

0 552 09178 2   £1.50

FIRE POWER
by Chris Dempster and Dave Tomkins

The true story of how two men looking for adventure ended up in Africa, alongside a handful of mercenaries from Europe and America, fighting a bloody last-ditch stand against Communist troops and tanks.

Of the estimated 150 mercenary volunteers who went to Angola to fight the Communists, over 60 remained there—in shallow graves, or as prisoners to be paraded in front of the world's television cameras. Chris Dempster and Dave Tomkins were just two of the men in Colonel Callan's ill-fated mercenary army.

FIRE POWER is the story of how they came to be fighting in Angola, and what happened to them when they were there. It is also a sensational glimpse of today's mercenary scene as portrayed by two real-life 'dogs of war'.

0 552 10807 3   £1.95

ASSIGNMENT GESTAPO
by Sven Hassel

Their more unorthodox weapons were lengths of steel wire
and knives with double-edged blades, and some of their most
prized possessions were gold teeth snatched from corpses...

The 'Disciplinary Regiment', a tank company in Hitler's
army—without a tank to its name—was fighting a brutal
war against the Russians. A bunch of hardened killers in
filthy rags, stinking to high heaven, this company was worth
an entire regiment of freshly laundered troops from Breslau.
Guerilla warfare on the Eastern front was for them a prelude
to the bloody massacre of Russian troops who'd attacked the
German reserves and occupied their headquarters. Then the
'Disciplinary Regiment' was sent to Hamburg, where their
next assignment was guard duty for the bestial Gestapo.

0   552   08779   3   £1.50

SS GENERAL
by Sven Hassel

The 27th Panzers in Hitler's Penal Reignment had fought
through the winter in the hell-hole that was Stalingrad. Now
there were few survivors from the last massive Russian attack.
Weary and nauseated by the horrors they's seen on the Russian front they crawled into a bunker near the banks of the
Volga. Hunger, they had discovered, was more demoralizing
than fear of defeat. Then the brutal SS General arrived....

0   552   113174   £1.50

BLITZFREEZE
by Sven Hassel

The Fuhrer's commands were simple—forward to Moscow!
And so the mighty Panzer regiments thundered into action—
killing, raping, burning their way across the great wastes of
Russia.

But this was to be the bloodiest of all Hitler's wars—a war
where Russian infantrymen threw themselves before the oncoming tanks, where women fought as savagely as men,
where German guns killed Germans and Russians alike, man-
gling them indiscriminately into tattered hunks of meat . . .

And finally Porta, Tiny, Barcelona, all of them—caring nothing for who should win the war—thinking only of their own
survival—began the long retreat—back through the corpse-
littered plains where blood and bodies were already frozen
beneath the winter ice . . .

0   552   09761   6   £1.25

A SELECTED LIST OF
CORGI TITLES

☐	11863 X	**The Sergeant I: Death Train**	*Gordon Davis*	95p
☐	11864 8	**The Sergeant 2: Hell Harbour**	*Gordon Davis*	95p
☐	11865 6	**The Sergeant 3: Bloody Bush**	*Gordon Davis*	95p
☐	10869 3	**The Wild Geese**	*Daniel Carney*	95p
☐	11168 6	**Court Martial**	*Sven Hassel*	£1.75
☐	10400 0	**The Bloody Road to Death**	*Sven Hassel*	£1.75
☐	09761 6	**Blitzfreeze**	*Sven Hassel*	£1.25
☐	09178 2	**Reign of Hell**	*Sven Hassel*	£1.50
☐	11317 4	**S.S. General**	*Sven Hassel*	£1.50
☐	08779 3	**Assignment Gestapo**	*Sven Hassel*	£1.50
☐	11414 6	**Liquidate Paris**	*Sven Hassel*	£1.50
☐	11411 1	**March Battalion**	*Sven Hassel*	£1.50
☐	11412 X	**Monte Cassino**	*Sven Hassel*	£1.50
☐	11377 8	**Comrades of War**	*Sven Hassel*	£1.50
☐	11259 3	**Wheels of Terror**	*Sven Hassel*	£1.75
☐	11417 0	**The Legion of the Damned**	*Sven Hassel*	£1.25
☐	10807 3	**Firepower**	*Chris Dempster & Dave Tomkins*	£1.95